THE DINNER PARTY

A PICK YOUR POISON ADVENTURE

FREIDA MCFADDEN

WARNING!!!!

DO NOT READ THIS BOOK
FROM BEGINNING TO END!

Yes, I know going straight from beginning to end is how you typically read books. But in this case, I'm going to ask you to do something a little different.

You're about to go on an adventure of your own choosing. You're going to start on the first page (this part is normal), but when you get to the end of each chapter, you're going to have to make a decision. If you decide on one path, the story will unfold in one way; if you decide on a different path, the story will unfold in a completely different way.

In other words, *you* get to pick your poison.

If you're the type of person who gets frustrated by characters in books making stupid decisions, this book is for you! YOU get to decide on your next move. The choice is entirely in your hands!

And if you die or end up on a super boring adventure, you can start all over again on page 1. There are 22 different endings in this book. You can (and should!) experience every single one of them, or else you can reach a single ending and quit, although that would be an extremely weird thing to do.

So if you're ready for an adventure, buckle your seatbelt and turn to the first chapter. And remember: the decisions are entirely in your hands!

Proceed to Chapter 1 (Page 1) if you dare...

1

YOU ARE BROKE.

It's not like you were rolling in dough before—being a diner waitress is hard work and low pay. You have been living paycheck to paycheck for years now, but things have recently taken a turn for the worse. You had some legal trouble in the last year, and although you avoided jail time, you're now overdrawn and in credit card debt. You are two weeks late paying the rent to your roommate, who is not the kind of nice and understanding roommate who will just be cool with that.

Also, you haven't had a boyfriend for 19 months, which has nothing to do with the broke thing, but it's yet another crappy thing about your life. Also, your roommate, Blair, *does* have a boyfriend, and the two of them are… *loud*.

On the plus side, at least things can't get any worse.

It's six o'clock on a Saturday night, and you are lying on the bed in your room, scrolling the internet on your phone for ideas on how to earn some extra money, while you try to tune out the sound of whatever Blair and her boyfriend are doing in the next room. It sounds like he's killing her. (Probably not—you should be so lucky.)

The internet is not proving terribly helpful in finding money-making ideas. It suggests working for Uber, but you don't have a car. It also suggests earning commissions by promoting products, but you have no social media following.

You have just clicked on a link to learn more about a promising site called OnlyFans when the door to your room suddenly flies open. It's Blair, who is not fond of knocking, but fortunately (or unfortunately), you're never doing anything in here that requires much privacy. She stands in the doorway in her boyfriend's oversized T-shirt, her golden blond hair mussed, her face flushed.

"Aha!" Blair shouts, pointing one of her manicured fingers at the small desk lamp on your nightstand. "I knew it! *This* is why our electricity bill is so high!"

The tiny lamp is the only source of light in your entire room. What does she want you to do? Sit here in pitch blackness?

"It's one light, Blair," you point out.

Blair plants her hands on her hips. "But you have light from your phone. Why do you need *another* light?"

You don't know what to say to that, so you keep your mouth shut, hoping she doesn't bring up the late rent payment.

"Also," she says, "you're two weeks late on the rent, Sloan."

Damn.

"I'm really sorry," you say. "I'll have it really soon. You know I've had some legal issues lately."

"I know, and that's why I've been trying to be *understanding*," Blair says in a voice that is not even the tiniest bit understanding. "But enough is enough! You can't live here for free, you know. Some of us work hard for our money."

You know for a fact that Blair's parents are paying the rent. She has a cushy job as something called a brand ambassador—not to be confused with any sort of diplomatic role—but it's not clear if she actually earns any money doing it. All you know is that people send her lots of products. And then she records herself taking them out of the package and looking excited about them. That's pretty much her whole job.

"I'm sorry," you say. "I know that I'm a little bit late on the rent, but I'll have it really soon." You won't. "Really." You're lying. "I 100% *promise*."

Blair glares down at you. "You'd better, Sloan. Because if you don't have the money for rent by tomorrow, you are seriously out of here."

"Tomorrow?" you squeak. "That's so soon…"

"I have somebody else who's interested in the room," she says. "So if you can't pay me, then I'm giving the room to her. Got it?"

Blair is always threatening you like that, and part of you thinks she's totally full of it. After all, it's not like she's going to really kick you out for being only two weeks late on the rent. Also, how dare she speak to you like that!

Still, there's no rental agreement, and if you lose this

room, you don't have anywhere else to go. It might be better to tread lightly here.

If you want to stand up to Blair, turn to Chapter 2 (page 5)

If you want to reassure Blair that you will have the rent on time, turn to Chapter 4 (page 10)

Important note: Chapter links should be used for the ebook, page numbers refer to the paperback ONLY!

2

"I KNOW MY RIGHTS!" YOU SPEAK UP. "YOU CAN'T JUST kick me out of here with one day's notice!"

Blair's eyes widen. You've known her for years, and in that time, you've never once stood up to her. Maybe now that you finally have, she'll respect you. You should've done this years ago!

Even better, Blair has flicked on the overhead lights in the room. After scrounging for electricity for the entire year you've lived here, she has finally given you light. That shows you've made the right decision by standing up to her.

"Thanks," you say.

But Blair isn't listening to you. She makes a beeline for the one small window near your bed and yanks it open. You're not sure why she did that, because it's pretty chilly out, and Blair always throws a fit about "wasting heat." But then her intentions become clear when she goes over to one of your dressers, scoops out an armful of clothing, and hurls it out your second-floor window.

"Hey!" You leap off the bed to stop her. "What are you doing?"

"You can't pay the rent," she says as she grabs another handful of panties and bras. "So I'm helping you vacate the premises."

You stand in front of the dresser, blocking her from taking any more clothing. That's when Blair's boyfriend, Griff, enters the room. Griff is about the size of a line-backer. Every time he takes a step, the entire room shakes.

"What's going on here?" Griff rumbles.

"We're helping Sloan move out," Blair explains. "Griff, would you please be a dear and help Sloan find the exit?"

Griff starts coming toward you, his tree trunk arms outstretched. Holy crap, this man is going to kill you if you don't get the hell out of here. He'll snap you in half like a twig.

"Okay, okay!" you cry, backing away from him. "I'll go."

You might as well. Half your stuff is already on the ground outside.

Turn to Chapter 3 (page 7)

3

By the time you get downstairs, you discover most of your belongings are scattered on the sidewalk outside the building. A bunch of your clothes landed in the snow that is still dotting the pavement. Thankfully, Blair was kind enough to throw down your luggage, so you start gathering items and shoving them in the bag.

That's when you notice a man has stopped and picked up one of your bracelets that has slipped into a crack in the sidewalk. And wow, this man is *handsome*. He has thick bronze hair, penetrating chocolate-brown eyes, and his body looks like it was sculpted by Michelangelo. His lips part in a smile that makes him even *more* gorgeous somehow. He holds out the bracelet to you.

"Is this yours?" he asks you.

Admittedly, your luck has been horrible over the last year. You nearly went to jail, you are dead broke, and now you are homeless. But you have a feeling that things are about to turn around in a big way.

"Why, yes," you say.

"Well…" The man's smile widens. "It's mine now. Finders keepers!"

He snaps his palm closed and shoves the bracelet in his pocket while you stare in disbelief.

"My girlfriend is going to *love* this," he informs you happily.

The man turns on his heel, then walks away, whistling to himself the whole time. Wow. So much for finding true love on the sidewalk.

It's a good thing you are so broke, because it means you don't own very much. It takes you about half an hour to gather all your belongings. You then create a makeshift fort for yourself in the alley next to the building. This is your home now.

While you're getting comfortable on the ground, a cat approaches you and nuzzles against you for warmth. She's actually quite beautiful, covered in a thick orange coat that is only slightly dirty. It feels like you've made a new best friend as you reach out and stroke her fur.

"Sorry, Kitty," you say to her. "I wish I had some food for you, but I don't even have food for myself."

As if she understands what you just said, she freaks out, letting out an eardrum-shattering howl. Then she lunges at you, first attempting to bite your leg, and when you try to disentangle her, she goes for the jugular. Her paw swipes at your hair, ripping out strands from your ponytail.

"What are you doing, Kitty?" you scream. "I was just petting you!"

Reasoning with this cat does not seem to be effective. She lunges for your leg again, and you have to abandon your fort. Embarrassingly, you're only barely able to outrun her. You hide behind some trash cans until she loses interest and wanders away.

Why have all your interactions with animals gone so badly lately?

Once the cat is safely out of sight, you return to your fort to lay down for the night. But you sleep with one eye open, worried the cat might return.

You were wrong. Things *could* get worse.

THE END

Want to try for a different ending? Turn back to Chapter 1 (page 1)!

4

You've never stood up to Blair before, but some instinct is telling you it's not a good idea. So instead, you nod obediently.

"Don't worry," you say. "I'll have every penny of the rent by tomorrow."

Somehow, you will figure out a way.

Blair gives you one last look, as if she doesn't quite believe you, which indicates that she's smarter than she seems. But she leaves the room, slamming the door behind her and plunging you back into semi-darkness.

Now what?

Before you can return to your internet search, your phone rings. You glance at the name on the screen: Avery. Avery is one of your oldest friends, who you've known since the two of you were in elementary school. You've gotten each other out of some bad jams over the years.

But on the other hand, Avery has gotten you *into* a lot of bad jams too.

You answer the phone: "Hello?"

"Sloan!" Avery sounds breathless, like she always does. "Thank God you picked up. Are you free tonight?"

"Yes…"

"Great! Want to make some money?"

Hope sparks in your chest. You had no idea how you were going to raise money for the rent, but Avery may just have the answer to your prayers. "Definitely. What do I have to do?"

While you wait for Avery to answer, you think about the list of things you're *not* willing to do. It's pretty short. You won't eat garbage, for example. Well, you might eat some kind of garbage. Like if some food was just hovering on the garbage, not quite inside the bin. But you wouldn't, for example, scrape out a banana peel from the bottom and eat that.

"It's a waitressing job," she says, which is great because you were literally about to eat garbage if you had to. "They told me they need an extra girl. It pays extremely well."

"How well?"

She tells you how much, and your jaw drops. That's enough to pay Blair for the rent. It's enough to pay next month's rent too.

"For a *waitressing* job?" you ask, feeling a bit skeptical. In your experience, if something sounds too good to be true, it probably is.

"Well," Avery amends, "it's a little more involved than that. You'll be gone the whole night, and it's a bit of a drive."

"A bit of a drive?"

"The house is at Peyton's Peak."

Peyton's Peak is a mountain about two hours from here. There are houses on the peak, most of them large estates owned by extremely wealthy and eccentric individuals who long for the isolation of living on a mountain. At this time of year, with all the snow on the ground, it will be a treacherous drive.

"Also," she adds, "the GPS doesn't work very well on the mountain. I'll have to give you written directions."

Written directions? Is she serious? What is this—the dinosaur era?

"I don't have a car," you remind Avery. "Can you give me a ride?"

"Unfortunately, I can't," she says. "I'm already here. But doesn't Blair have a car? Could you borrow it?"

Blair has, on occasion, allowed you to borrow her car, which was also a gift from her parents. If you tell her that you need it to get the rent money, there is a reasonable chance she'll let you borrow it.

"So?" Avery asks eagerly. "Are you interested?"

This job seems like the answer to your prayers. But at the same time, there's something in your gut telling you this isn't a good idea. Are you really this desperate for money?

To take the waitressing job, turn to Chapter 7 (page 16)

To decline the job because it will almost certainly get you killed, turn to Chapter 5 (page 13)

5

———

"I'm sorry," you tell Avery. "It just sounds really sketchy. I don't think it's a good idea."

"Are you sure?" she presses you. "That's a lot of money for one night of waitressing. And I know you're short on cash."

She's right. But your gut is telling you it would be a mistake to take that job. Somehow, you'll find a way to raise rent money.

"Thanks for thinking of me," you say, "but I'm going to have to say no."

"Your loss."

You hang up the phone, and for a moment, you wonder if you've made a mistake. You really need that money.

Continue to Chapter 6 (page 14)

6

You're not going to take any unnecessary risks. One way or another, you'll figure out how to scrape together the funds to pay the rent. And even though she told you she wants you out by tomorrow if you don't pay, you're sure Blair doesn't really mean it. After all, what's she going to do? Grab all your clothes from your drawers and throw them out the window? Then force you to live in a makeshift fort in the alley next to the building?

Of course not. That's ridiculous.

You take a break from thinking about money. Instead, you decide to spend the night in your room, curled up with a novel, reading about a character who made more interesting choices than you just did.

Tomorrow, you will look into that OnlyFans site. You've always had an interest in HVAC units, ceiling fans, and artisanal desk fans. This could be the beginning of a great new career.

THE END

Want to try for a different ending? Turn back to
Chapter 1 (page 1)!

7

"FINE," YOU TELL AVERY, "I'LL TAKE THE JOB."

"That's wonderful!" She sounds happier than anyone rightfully should after convincing a friend to take a waitressing job. "You won't regret this, Sloan."

That remains to be seen.

First, you have to convince Blair to lend you her car. That will be no easy task, but it's the only way you're going to be able to drive out to Peyton's Peak. Even if you could afford it, no Uber will go out that far.

You knock on the door to Blair's bedroom. Based on the sounds coming from inside, you're definitely interrupting them in the middle of something, but given that those sounds are always going on, you don't have much of a choice. You hear swearing behind the door, then Blair yanks it open, looking annoyed.

"What is it, Sloan?"

"Um." You wring your hands together. "I was wondering if I could borrow your car tonight?"

Blair looks at you like you just asked her to promise

you her firstborn. She folds her arms across her chest. "Why?"

"I got a waitressing job," you explain. "But it's out at Peyton's Peak. It's a hike, but it'll pay enough that I can give you the rent tomorrow."

Blair considers this. She doesn't like to lend you her car, but she wants that rent money.

"Fine," she finally says, "but if there's so much as a *scratch* on my car at the end of the night, you're going to be very sorry."

You do not doubt that. But you're an excellent driver, so you're not too worried. "Thank you! I promise I'll be very careful."

Avery didn't mention if you'll be expected to change into a uniform, so you dress in a pair of black slacks and a white dress shirt that will hopefully be appropriate for serving an upscale dinner party. You tug on a coat because the weather is still chilly, and it's only going to get colder as the night goes on. You pull your black hair back into a simple ponytail.

You feel strangely nervous about this job, which is odd, because you have waitressed thousands of times before. But you can't seem to shake the uneasy feeling in the pit of your stomach. Still, you had a chance to say no, and you didn't take it. It's time to get going.

It's colder outside than you thought. You zip up your coat to your throat as you walk down the steps of your building. As soon as you reach the bottom step, a cat materializes from the alley by your building. She nuzzles her head against your leg and looks up at you hopefully. She's clearly looking for food, and based on how scrawny she is, it's slim pickings around here.

You *love* animals. Sometimes you think you prefer them to people. On any other night, you'd scrounge up some food for this hungry cat, but you shouldn't be dawdling. You told Avery you were going to head over right away, and it's a long drive to Peyton's Peak. There's no time to worry about a stray cat.

But the cat looks so hungry. How could you leave her without at least giving her a nibble of something to eat?

To go upstairs and get food for the cat, turn to Chapter 8 (page 19)

To head straight to your car, turn to Chapter 9 (page 21)

8

YES, IT'S IMPORTANT TO HAVE MONEY FOR THE RENT, BUT you're not going to ignore a hungry animal. You'll take five minutes to feed this cat, and then you can be on your way.

You hurry back upstairs, and thankfully, Blair and her boyfriend Griff are still in their bedroom. You yank open the fridge and scan the contents. There isn't much in there, besides a bunch of Chinese food leftover containers. You grab the first one you see and pop it open. Hopefully, cats like kung pow chicken.

You palm a few pieces of chicken, then hurry back downstairs. The cat is waiting for you, meowing plaintively. She looks like she's starving. You're glad you decided to take a few minutes to feed her.

You sit on the steps of your building and rip a little piece of the chicken off for the cat. She gobbles it up in one bite, then looks at you for more. Apparently, cats *do* like kung pow chicken. You give her the rest, and within a few seconds, all the chicken is gone. After she finishes, she rubs against you gratefully, and you pet her soft fur. What a sweet cat.

Now that you've done a good deed, it's time to get on the road!

Turn to Chapter 9 (page 21)

9

Blair's father bought her a silver Audi as a graduation present, and you are going to do your best not to bust it up during this drive. You do not doubt that Blair will make good on her promise to make your life a living hell if anything happens to that car.

You slide into the driver's seat and start up the engine. Oh wow, this car has both a heated seat *and* a heated steering wheel. All it needs is a toilet, and this car would be better than any place you have ever lived in your entire life. It will be a shame to hand it back over to Blair at the end of the evening.

Maybe you should steal it. *This car* can be your new home. It's a victimless crime—Blair's father can just buy her another one.

No, you need to stop slobbering over this car. You've got a job to do.

You get on the road, driving in the direction of Peyton's Peak. You use GPS, recognizing that when you get closer to the estate, the GPS won't work anymore.

You have a sheet of scribbled directions that you will use when the signal cuts out. You're especially worried that your phone likely won't work at that point either. What if you get lost?

Once again, you wonder if you're making a mistake taking this job. A remote mountain location? No GPS signal? A paycheck that is far more than any waitress job should rightfully pay? This is *super* sketchy. But you can't change your mind anymore. You're doing this.

While you're still in the city, there are lots of cars around. After all, it's Saturday night, and everyone but you is out having a good time. But after you get out of the city, the roads become less crowded, and the further you drive in the direction of the mountain, the more desolate it becomes. At some point, you realize that 15 minutes have passed by and you haven't seen any other cars.

That's okay, though. You don't mind being alone, and it's actually nice to be on this quiet drive. It gives you time to think.

For example, you can think about your legal problems. Your empty bank account. Your complete lack of a love life.

Ugh, this sucks. What's on the radio?

The rock songs distract you while you continue on the deserted road. After you've been driving for a little over an hour, you notice something on the side of the road. You've got your brights on, but it's still very hard to see. It's only when you get closer that you can make out what it is.

It's a man. He's standing all alone next to the road, his thumb stuck up in the air, a duffel bag by his side.

A hitchhiker.

The hitchhiker is dressed inappropriately for the weather in a light jacket—he must be freezing. How long has he been out there? There aren't many cars going by, and if you don't stop, he could be there for hours.

But what can you do? You can't stop. You're not on a road trip—you have to get to this dinner party so you can earn enough money to pay your rent. And even if you didn't have anywhere to go, it's not a good idea to stop for a hitchhiker. You're a young woman, all alone in the middle of nowhere. It could be dangerous.

Plus, this hitchhiker looks a little sketchy. He's got unkempt hair and a big bushy beard. There's something a little wild about his expression.

Then again, this poor man has been standing out in the cold for God knows how long. How could you just drive by?

To stop for the hitchhiker, turn to Chapter 10 (page 24)

To keep driving, turn to Chapter 14 (page 34)

10

YOU HAVE TO STOP FOR THE HITCHHIKER. IT'S THE decent thing to do. You can't let a man freeze to death waiting for a ride.

You pull over along the side of the road. A smile curls across the hitchhiker's face, and you're glad you made this decision. Helping a fellow human is the right thing to do. Humans are almost as good as animals.

"Thank you *so* much," the hitchhiker says as he climbs into the car beside you. He looks to be around fifty, with fine lines around his eyes and a lot of gray in his bushy beard, but not quite as much in his wild hair.

"Of course," you say. "How long were you waiting out there?"

"Two hours."

"Oh wow." You feel a rush of sympathy for this man. "Well, I'm heading toward Peyton Peak. Where are you going?"

"Actually, that's perfect," he says. "I'm going to stay

with a friend just at the base of the mountain. So you can drop me off right before you head up to the peak."

"Happy to," you say. "I'm Sloan, by the way."

He smiles, revealing a mouthful of slightly yellow but relatively intact teeth. "Jasper."

You didn't realize how lonely you were during this drive until Jasper showed up. You're grateful for the company, and the two of you strike up a conversation. Jasper tells you that he recently lost his wife, and ever since, he's been drifting from state to state, taking odd jobs when he can find them.

"Lorna always wanted to see the country," he says, "and she never got around to it while she was still alive. So now is her chance."

You look over your shoulder, checking to make sure the ghost of Lorna isn't in the backseat. "What do you mean?"

He pats his duffel bag. "I carry her ashes everywhere I go. That way everything I see, she sees too."

That's really sweet. A little creepy, sure, but mostly sweet. As long as the duffel bag just contains Lorna's ashes and not... well, Lorna.

After another 20 minutes of driving, you reach a turn-off on the main road. Jasper points to it. "That's me," he says.

You slow down, squinting at the dark road. It's an unlit, narrow path that is paved, but just barely. It's badly overgrown with weeds and branches. You pull over, not sure what to do.

"It's not far from here," Jasper says. "Maybe a 15-

minute walk. But I won't say no if you wouldn't mind giving me a ride."

You hesitate. You hate the idea of kicking Jasper out and letting him walk down that cold, dark path all by himself. You've made good time on your drive, and you have time for the quick detour to the cabin. But when you start to turn the steering wheel, you hesitate. Something in your gut is telling you it would be a mistake to go down that narrow road.

But that's silly. Isn't it?

To give Jasper a ride directly to his cabin, turn to Chapter 12 (page 29)

To drop him off right here, turn to Chapter 11 (page 27)

11

"Sorry, I'd better get going," you tell Jasper. "I'm supposed to be at this dinner party. I don't want to be late."

"Oh." He looks disappointed, but nods in understanding. "I see. Well, thank you for taking me this far. You're very kind."

"No problem."

You sit there, waiting for Jasper to exit your car. But he isn't moving. He's just sitting there, staring at you, a strange look in his eyes. The light of the full moon makes the white hairs in his beard almost look like tiny worms.

"Um," you say, "I really have to get going. Unless you're coming to the dinner party?" You laugh, although it comes out choked. "Seriously, though. I don't want to be late."

But he doesn't budge. Instead, he reaches out his large hands and wraps them around your throat.

You try to scream, but you can't because his hands

are cutting off your windpipe. His grip tightens until you start to see spots, and then your vision fades entirely.

You're going to die. This man is going to kill you.

You are losing consciousness, and your final thought before you succumb to death is that if only you hadn't picked up this hitchhiker, your night would have gone completely differently.

THE END

Want to try for a different ending? Turn back to Chapter 1 (page 1)!

12

"I can take you to the cabin," you say. "No problem."

"Thank you," Jasper says. "You're so kind."

You *are* kind, and you've earned some good karma by picking up the hitchhiker. It's not your fault you've had a run of bad luck lately, but hopefully, that's about to change. You can *feel* it.

You turn down the dark, narrow road, relying on the beam of the headlights to see what's in front of you. You drive slowly because it's still hard to see, and the path is only somewhat paved. If anything happens to this car, Blair will definitely kill you. You're getting worried that one of the branches could scratch the car, and you start to think this was a mistake, but it's too late now.

After a few minutes, you come across a cabin in a clearing. You pull up in front of it and throw the car into park.

"Well," you say, "here you are!"

"Thank you so much, Sloan," Jasper says. "You don't know how much I appreciate this."

"I'm happy to help."

He glances over at the cabin, then back at you. "Listen, would you like to come in for a minute? I know you've got to be somewhere, but you've obviously been driving a long time. You should take a minute to stop and stretch your legs. Have a cup of tea."

You look at the time display on the dashboard. You *are* making very good time. "Well…"

"Come on," Jasper urges you. "It's the least I can do for you after you picked me up and brought me here."

"Well…"

To follow Jasper into his cabin, turn to Chapter 13 (page 31)

To continue on your way, turn to Chapter 11 (page 27)

13

You've been sitting in this car for almost 90 minutes. Your back is starting to ache, and you have a cramp in your right calf. It would certainly be nice to stretch your legs a bit. And you're making excellent time. There's no point in being early, is there?

"Sure," you say, "I'd love to come in for a minute."

You climb out of the car and are horrified to discover that there are long scratches from the branches running all along the doors. Oh God, Blair is going to *kill* you. But you'll worry about that later.

Jasper leads you to the cabin. But as you get closer, you notice that it's far more run-down than you realized. In fact, it almost looks abandoned. You wonder if it was a good idea to agree to come inside, but at this point, it's too late to change your mind. You are already committed to this choice.

The door rattles on its hinges as Jasper pulls it open, holding it for you like a gentleman. Unfortunately, the inside isn't any better than the outside. The cabin contains only sparse furniture, including a waterlogged sofa, an overturned wooden chair, a bookcase that has one shelf filled with spiral notebooks and another filled with dusty old dolls. There's also a fireplace, which is unlit—the cabin is freezing. In the corner is a small pile of firewood, with an ax balanced on top of it.

How are you supposed to sit and have some tea? There isn't even a table! And the stove is covered in rust, as are all the pots.

"You said your friend lives here?" you ask dubiously.

"That's right," Jasper says vaguely.

You want to ask if his friend ever cleans, but that would be rude. Still, this cabin looks abandoned. You turn to Jasper, not sure if he's thinking the same thing, but he's ignoring you. His gaze is directed at the fireplace.

"You going to get the fire going?" you ask. It's the one thing in this cabin that looks like it works.

"Sure," he says as he walks toward the fireplace. "Good idea."

Part of you wants to help Jasper get the fire going, but a bigger part of you wants to get the hell out of here.

"You know," you say, "it really is getting late. I should probably get back to my car and head up the mountain."

Jasper reaches down for the pile of firewood. You expect him to grab a couple of logs to toss onto the fire, but instead, he picks up the ax.

"Um," you say. "What are you doing with that?"

You ask such stupid questions.

Jasper lets out what sounds like a war cry. He comes running at you with the ax raised above his head. You turn around and start to run in the opposite direction.

You make it out the door and all the way to the car before Jasper catches up with you. He lets out another cry and brings down the ax. He misses you by an inch, the blade coming down on the passenger's side door, resulting in a huge indentation.

"Not the car!" you screech. Blair is going to be *livid*.

The good news is his next swing of the ax doesn't do further damage to the car. The bad news is that the ax hits you square in the chest, slicing cleanly through skin and bone.

You crumple to the ground in a puddle of your own blood. As you lay dying, you think to yourself that if only you hadn't gotten out of the car, everything would have been different.

THE END

Want to try for a different ending? Turn back to
Chapter 1 (page 1)!

14

UNFORTUNATELY, AS MUCH AS YOU WOULD LOVE TO HELP out the hitchhiker by giving him a ride, you just don't have time. So you leave the poor man on the side of the road, with his thumb stuck in the air. Hopefully, someone else will come by soon and take pity on him.

You keep driving on the empty road. Eventually, you hit the base of the mountain and start the treacherous drive upward. Shortly after you begin your ascent, the GPS on your phone cuts out as promised, so all you've got are Avery's directions lying on the seat beside you.

The road up the mountain is dangerously narrow. Even one wrong turn could take you off the edge, plummeting to your death. Or worse, you could wreck Blair's car. You drive very, very carefully. It's slow going, but due to the lack of traffic, you're ahead of schedule. Better to be safe than sorry.

After about 15 minutes of navigating the winding road, you come to a fork.

You pull over and turn on the lights in the car. You

check the directions in the seat beside you, scanning for a mention of a fork in the road. Naturally, there's nothing there.

You grab your phone, hoping to call her and clarify, but of course, your cell service is out. It looks like you're on your own.

You turn out the lights to improve your visibility. You peer out the windshield, trying to make heads or tails of the situation. There are two directions you can go: left or right.

On the left, the path seems to go inward, almost *into* the mountain. It must be colder on this path, since the road is caked with snow that hasn't been entirely cleared away. It certainly does not look like a road that has seen many cars recently.

On the right, the road becomes narrower. Almost too narrow for Blair's car, which is not exactly wide. There's also a diamond-shaped sign mounted at the right fork, and the red lettering in all caps states: "SHARP TURNS AHEAD." And then a second sign underneath that says, "PROCEED WITH CAUTION!"

Well, it looks like you have two terrible options. Since Avery's directions aren't at all helpful, you have to make a decision.

To go left, turn to Chapter 15 (page 36)

To go right, turn to Chapter 32 (page 77)

15

THE CAUTIONARY SIGNS HAVE SPOOKED YOU, SO YOU decide to go left. You figure any path that doesn't have a warning label is more promising.

You just wish somebody had cleared away the snow.

As you continue to drive, the road gets even more slippery. The snow is piled up on the ground, and even though Blair's car has four-wheel drive, it is struggling. Even worse, when you stop again to check Avery's directions, they don't seem to be matching up with anything you are seeing. None of the roads are labeled. It's a bad sign.

You're worried that you have gone the wrong way.

At this point, you should probably turn around and go back where you came from. But the road is so narrow and slippery that turning around will be challenging. So you keep moving forward, hoping that the road will clear and that you will suddenly arrive at the house for the dinner party, right on time.

Unfortunately, the further you go, the more obvious

it is that's not going to happen. You have taken the wrong path, and you must turn around.

You slow to a halt on the snowy road. You put the car in reverse, but when you try to back up, you can't. Sighing, you put the car back in drive, but when you press on the gas, you don't budge.

This time, you floor it. The car's wheels spin frantically, but you're not moving forward. The momentum must have been propelling you forward, and once you stopped, you lost that momentum. You're now stuck.

You try a few more times to floor the gas, but it doesn't work. There is obviously a bunch of snow in front of your car, and unless you clear it away by hand, you're not going anywhere. So much for being early to the dinner party.

You start to open the door to the car, but as soon as it opens a crack, you hear a sound. It sounds like the howl of a wolf in the distance.

You freeze. The wolf sounds like it's far away, but not *that* far away. It occurs to you that there are almost certainly wild animals roaming around these parts in the middle of the night. It might not be safe to get out of the car. If you're inside, at least you can't get eaten.

But what are you supposed to do? You don't have enough gas to keep the car running all night long, and if you stay here, you're going to freeze to death.

To get out of the car, turn to Chapter 17 (page 40)

To stay in the car, turn to Chapter 16 (page 38)

16

You decide the best thing to do is to stay in the car. There are some scary noises outside, and at least in here, you'll be safe. And you have almost half a tank of gas. Maybe you'll make it through the night. If you don't return home by the morning, Blair will almost certainly send out a search party to find her Audi.

Just to be safe, you keep the heat on low and turn the radio off.

It takes a little over an hour for the gas to run out. You thought you'd have longer somehow. The car engine dies, and you are left in your dark car with no heat. You hug your body for warmth, but this mountain is extremely cold—well below freezing. You can see puffs of your breath in the air. If only you had brought something more than your light jacket. A hat would have definitely been nice.

As the hours go by, the temperature continues to drop precipitously. You had no idea how cold it could get on a mountain. You consider getting out of the car, but when you try the door, it is frozen shut. Even if you could somehow dig yourself out, you have no gas left in the car. You had your chance to get out, and you missed it.

At two in the morning, a miracle occurs. All of a sudden, you feel *warm* again. At first, you are sure that the heat has magically turned back on, but no, the engine is still dead. So why are you warm again all of a sudden? You're not just warm—you're hot. Like you're burning up!

You strip off your coat because it's way too hot in this car for a coat. Vaguely, in the back of your head, you remember reading about how when you're freezing to death, the muscles controlling the peripheral blood vessels that have been keeping heat close to the body become exhausted and give out. This causes a sudden rush of warm blood from the body's core to the extremities that can make you feel like you're burning up. It's the last fatal stage of hypothermia.

That isn't what is happening to you, though. Is it?

But before you worry about it, a gentle cloudiness comes over you. Gosh, it's so nice and warm in this car. You're just going to shut your eyes for a few minutes. When you wake up, it'll be morning, and you'll be safe to find your way home.

THE END

Want to try for a different ending? Turn back to Chapter 1 (page 1)!

17

As much as it scares you to leave the safety of your vehicle, you don't want to freeze to death. Your only hope is to try to dig yourself out so you can keep moving.

You wrench open the car door and step outside. The wind is brutal. You brace yourself against it as you step around to the front of the car, which is blocked by a mound of snow. You're also horrified to discover that the ice has scratched up the side of the car—Blair is going to *kill* you.

Now what are you going to do? It's not like you have a shovel. You could check the trunk, but you're pretty sure Blair isn't the kind of person who keeps a shovel in her trunk.

Maybe you should have stayed inside the car. Maybe that would've been a smarter decision.

Just as you're contemplating whether you should get back in the car and wait with the heat on, you hear a loud thump from behind you. It's loud enough that the whole earth seems to tremble, and then a second, louder thump echoes through the night air.

What the hell is that?

You should *not* have gotten out of the car—you made a grave mistake. You've got to get back inside, if it isn't already too late. You don't know what that sound was, but you know you are in terrible danger.

You turn around, your heart pounding. And now you get an eyeful of a terrible creature—like something out of your nightmares. It's at least twice as large as you are, and covered in white fur. It has sharp yellow fangs and angry dark eyes. You have never seen anything that terrifying in your entire life. It feels like your heart is about to explode out of your chest.

And then everything goes black.

Turn to Chapter 18 (page 42)

18

YOU WAKE UP ON THE FRIGID, HARD GROUND.

You have no idea where you are. You only know that you are cold, but warmer than you were when you were standing outside your car. You blink a few times, trying to focus. You're someplace dark, but there's a flickering light coming from about six feet away—a fire. That must be what's providing the warmth.

And then you realize where you are:

Inside a cave.

How did you get here? You only remember that terrifying creature rushing towards you, his claws drawn. Then the next thing you knew, you were opening your eyes in this place.

The creature must have brought you here as his prisoner.

You struggle into a sitting position, rubbing your head, which feels sore. You're dimly aware of a noise coming from behind you. A grunting sound.

It turns out you're not alone in this cave.

You whirl around, expecting to come face-to-face with that monster. But the monster isn't here. Instead, you find a man bound and gagged on the ground about ten feet away from you. He has wild hair and a bushy beard. He looks strangely familiar…

Wait. Is that the hitchhiker you saw on your way here? The one you didn't pick up, because you didn't want to be late to the dinner party?

Yes! It is!

Apparently, the furry yeti monster has taken both you and the hitchhiker as his prisoners. You're not sure what his plan is, but you wouldn't be surprised if you end up being his dinner. But the strange (well, *strangest*) part is that only the hitchhiker has been physically restrained. His wrists and ankles are bound with rope, while yours have been left free. The monster probably thinks that you won't be a threat to him because you're a woman. What a sexist monster.

The hitchhiker grunts more loudly, trying to get your attention. Your legs still feel too weak to stand, so you crawl across the cold floor to where he's lying. He has a cloth tied around his mouth that serves as a gag. You pull it down so that he can speak to you.

"Thank God!" he gasps. "When you were just lying there, I thought for sure you were… well, you know."

You rub your sore scalp, wondering if that's why the monster didn't tie you up. Maybe he, too, thought that you were dead.

"You've got to untie me," the hitchhiker says urgently. "He took off about 15 minutes ago, but he could be back at any time. We've got to get out of here. *Now*."

"Right," you say, but then you hesitate.

"Come *on*," the hitchhiker urges you. "We don't have much time. If he gets back here, he'll kill us both for sure."

He's right. You're both stuck in the cave of a terrifying yeti monster, who could probably kill you both with one hand tied behind his back. Your only chance to survive is to get the hell out of here.

Yet…

There's something about this situation that seems off. Why is only the hitchhiker tied up? It doesn't make sense.

But you can't just leave him here, can you? That would be even worse than when you drove by him on the road. You're certainly not heartless.

To untie the hitchhiker, turn to Chapter 19 (page 45)

To keep the rope in place, turn to Chapter 20 (page 48)

19

THE HITCHHIKER IS RIGHT. YOU'VE GOT TO UNTIE HIM and get out of here as quickly as you can. As soon as that creature returns, you are both toast. There's no way you can leave him here for dead.

You crawl around to reach the ties behind his back. You don't have a knife, but you're able to work the ties free that bind his wrists. Once those are free, he's able to help you get his ankles untied. Now unshackled, he sits there on the ground, rubbing his red, chapped wrists.

"Thank you," he breathes. "Thank you so much."

"Come on." You scramble to your feet, acutely aware of the fact that the monster could return at any moment. "Let's get out of here."

"Right." His voice has an odd intonation all of a sudden, like he isn't quite human himself. "We should go."

He gets to his feet much too slowly. You don't know why he is suddenly acting like you have all the time in the world when a yeti monster is literally about to come back any second and eat you.

"Which way is out?" you ask him.

He doesn't answer right away, but after a few beats, he points a finger to the right.

"Are you sure?" you ask.

"Pretty sure," he says, not sounding sure at all.

Given that anything else would be a complete guess, you decide to trust his sense of direction. You do feel a breeze as you start traveling right, which makes you think that it might lead outdoors. But at the same time, you're moving away from the light and heat of the fire, which means that it's getting colder and darker.

"I can barely see," you breathe.

"Yes," the hitchhiker agrees. "Me either."

"I wish we had a light."

"Actually," the hitchhiker says, "I have a lighter in my pocket."

"Great!"

You stand there as he fumbles around in his pocket for the lighter. After a few seconds, you hear a click as the lighter ignites. A tiny orb of fire illuminates his face, making his eyes look almost demonic.

"By the way, Sloan," he says in a low voice, "did I ever thank you for untying me?"

Wait. Did you tell him your name was Sloan? You must have, because how else would he know? But at this moment, you can't remember ever telling him your name, and that fact is almost as terrifying as the yeti monster.

"I am *so* glad you untied me," he hisses at you.

And then he smiles.

You scream as the flame goes out, just as the hitch-hiker's fingers wrap around your throat. As he squeezes the life out of you, you can't help but think to yourself that if only you hadn't untied him, everything would have been different.

THE END

Want to try for a different ending? Turn back to Chapter 1 (page 1)!

20

SOMETHING IN YOUR GUT IS TELLING YOU NOT TO UNTIE the hitchhiker. You're not sure why, but you don't want to undo the ropes binding his arms and legs until you have a better idea what's going on here.

"Hang on," you say. "Give me a minute."

"A minute?" he repeats. "Didn't you hear me? That yeti monster is coming back here to *kill* us. You're never going to get out of here without my help, you know."

He might be right, but still, you aren't sure if you should untie him. Something in your gut is urging you to wait.

"I'm sure we have time," you say.

"We don't." He struggles fruitlessly against the restraints. That yeti sure knows how to tie a knot. "Come *on*. You're not really going to leave me here like this, are you?"

"Um..."

"Please!" He stops struggling as his eyes lock with yours. "You've *got* to let me out. He'll kill me! *Please!*"

Okay, one last chance…

To untie the hitchhiker, turn to Chapter 19 (page 45)

To keep the ties in place, turn to Chapter 21 (page 50)

21

"I'M SORRY," YOU SAY. "I'M NOT UNTYING YOU YET."

The hitchhiker jerks his body, trying to work himself free. "I can't believe this! You... you bitch!"

Well, you're definitely not untying him now.

You raise the gag again and stuff it in the hitchhiker's mouth, so you don't have to listen to him swearing at you. Then you get to your feet and look around the cave.

There is a small fire in the center of the clearing, which is providing the light and the heat. Other than that, there's not much here. You do notice some sort of makeshift bed formed from old leaves. Is that where the monster sleeps?

Well, the hitchhiker is right about one thing. You've got to get the hell out of here. And you don't have much time.

A slight breeze is coming from the right. That must be the direction of the cave entrance—or, at least, you hope so. If you can escape from here, hopefully you'll be able to find your way back to the car. As soon as you find that car, you're taking off.

You start down the tunnel to the right, but before you get more than a few feet, you hear a roar coming from within the tunnel. That's quickly followed by the same resounding footsteps that you heard when you were by your car.

Oh no. He's back.

You made a mistake. You should have run while you had the chance. Now it's too late. The monster is going to eat you up and then devour the hitchhiker for dessert. (Or perhaps the hitchhiker will be the main course, and you'll be dessert. He seems a bit more substantial.)

You search the cave for a potential weapon. There is a large rock in the corner, which looks like it could do some damage. But then again, the monster is so much bigger than you. It doesn't seem like fighting it would be possible—not unless you have a gun.

Maybe it would be better to try to reason with him. You can't assume that he speaks any sort of English, but perhaps you could do some sort of pantomime to show that you are friendly. Or at least that you don't taste very good.

Whatever you decide, you only have one chance to get it right. If you try to fight the creature and lose, he will almost certainly eat you.

To fight the creature, turn to Chapter 22 (page 52)

To try to reason with it, turn to Chapter 23 (page 55)

22

YOU'VE NEVER BEEN ONE TO TAKE YOUR FATE LYING down. If that monster wants to eat you, he's going to have to work for it.

You pick up the rock and crouch in the clearing. It occurs to you that you could untie the hitchhiker, because two against one might be better odds, but you just don't trust him. Besides, if the hitchhiker is available as a ready snack, then the monster won't need to eat you.

The thumping noises are growing louder and louder. *Thump thump thump.* You're not sure which is louder—the footsteps or your heart. Either way, in a minute, you're going to come face-to-face with the monster.

You see his imposing shadow before he comes into view. He lets out a resounding roar that shakes the entire cave to its core. You are so scared, you nearly drop the rock.

And then a second later, there he is.

This is the first opportunity you've had to get a good look at him—out by your car, you didn't have much of a chance. He's about eight feet tall and covered head to toe in white fur. Except, of course, for his fingers, which are a deep purple. His nose is nothing more than two breathing holes in the center of his face, and his eyes are two endless dark abysses. The glow of the fire provides just enough light to make out his sharp yellow teeth. As you stare at him, you finally realize what you're looking at.

This monster is the *abominable snowman*. The monster from the *legends*.

But you don't even have a chance to be awed by this earthshattering discovery. If there was ever a chance to fight this creature, it's now, while you still have the element of surprise. You raise the rock high over your head, and you run at him as fast as you can. The creature sees what you're trying to do and lets out a furious roar.

When you get within striking distance, you make your move. You hurl the rock at the creature as hard as you can. You gasp with the effort.

The rock finds its target in the creature's right leg. Except even though you hurled it with all your might, the rock bounces harmlessly off of him. That giant rock did *nothing*. You may as well have thrown a pebble at him.

So much for fighting him.

The monster lets out another roar that shakes the walls of the cave. And then a second. And a third. But then, when he lets out a snort, you finally realize that he is not, in fact, growling at you in fury.

He is *laughing*.

Turn to Chapter 24 (page 58)

23

You've never been much of a fighter. And even if you were, you have no chance against that giant beast that is twice your size. Your best chance is to try to gain his sympathy so that he might let you go.

You wait in the clearing, planning out what you want to say to him. Luckily, you're so broke that you haven't been able to eat much lately—you can make the argument that you'll be far too lean and stringy for him to enjoy. Plus, the hitchhiker is still tied up and available as a delicious alternative.

You stand there, terrified, as the thumping of the monster's feet on the ground grows louder and louder. You're not sure which is louder, the footsteps or your heart. Either way, in a minute, you're going to come face-to-face with the beast.

You see his imposing shadow before he comes into view. He lets out a low roar as he bumps his way into the clearing, and it takes a few moments before he comes into view. And when he does, you are so scared, you nearly pee your pants.

This is the first chance you've had to get a good look at him—out by your car, you didn't have much of a chance. He's about eight feet tall and covered head to toe in white fur. Except, of course, for his fingers, which are a deep purple. His nose is nothing more than two breathing holes in the center of his face, and his eyes are two endless dark abysses. The glow of the fire provides just enough light to make out his sharp yellow teeth. As you stare at him, you finally realize what you're looking at.

This monster is the *abominable snowman*. The monster from the *legends*.

You don't have any time to waste. If you hesitate, he's going to scoop you up, pop you in his mouth, and gulp you down in one bite. He'll be licking his fingers before you can even get a word out.

Impulsively, you fall to your knees. "Kind sir," you say, "I am here to throw myself at your mercy."

The abominable snowman just looks at you. But he doesn't lick his lips or anything like that, so you plow forward.

"I know that you can do whatever you want with me," you continue, "but if you could find it in your heart to spare me, I can... Well, I'm not entirely sure what you'd like me to do. I could..." You glance around the cave. "I could tidy up. I could organize some of the rocks over there! I could help you build other snowmen, in case you want to make an army or something. I could, um, build you a snowwoman, in case you're, um, lonely?"

You can't tell if he understands one word coming out of your mouth. For all you know, your entire speech just sounded like unintelligible grunts to him. Also, like with most men, his expression is incredibly hard to read. In that sense, he sort of reminds you of your last boyfriend, Josh, which doesn't make you like him any better.

And then the abominable snowman lets out another roar that shakes the walls of the cave. Your heart sinks. None of this is getting through. Despite your best efforts, this monster is going to kill you.

But then his shoulders start to shake. And that's when you realize that he is not, in fact, growling at you.

He is *laughing*.

Turn to Chapter 24 (page 58)

24

"Is this *funny*?" you ask.

The abominable snowman has stopped laughing. He shakes his head, but under all that fur, his lips are twitching. It seems like the snowman doesn't want to eat you, but instead is mocking you, which might be even worse. Well, no, actually, wanting to eat you is definitely worse. But this is bad too.

"Why are you laughing?" you demand to know.

Because…" His voice startles you. It is a low rumble, but somehow not as threatening as you thought it would be. His English is perfect. "You humans *always* think we want to eat you, like you're *so* delicious. Seriously, you are so full of yourselves. I'll have you know that human beings are actually quite stringy and unpleasant to consume."

Well, that's a relief. Although you have to wonder how he knows that. "Then why did you kidnap me?"

"I didn't *kidnap* you." The yeti rolls his eyes. "You passed out in front of your car. If I left you there, you would have frozen to death. I *saved* you." He adds, "You're *welcome*."

Well, that could be true. Now that you think of it, you don't actually remember the abominable snowman knocking you out or attacking you. All you remember is being terrified, and then everything went black.

"Wait," you say. "What about the man tied up over there? You can't tell me you don't mean any harm to him!"

The monster's gaze hardens. "That is true."

Aha! You knew a creature this terrifying had to be dangerous.

"The truth is," the creature says, "soon after I brought you here, I found that man skulking around the cave. I followed him inside, and he was about to smash you in the head with a giant rock. I tied him up to keep him from killing you."

Could that be true? You look over your shoulder at the hitchhiker bound and gagged on the ground, grunting and straining at his bindings. The truth is, you had a bad feeling about that hitchhiker. It's why you decided not to untie him.

The abominable snowman may have just saved your life. And you're not quite sure how to feel about it.

Turn to Chapter 25 (page 60)

25

THE FIRE IS WANING, SO THE ABOMINABLE SNOWMAN ambles over and throws a few logs into it. The logs are wider than your legs, but he heaves them into his strong arms with barely a grunt. If he wanted to hurt you, there would be no way you could stop him, but it's clear that's not his goal.

"Thank you," you blurt out.

The creature looks over his shoulder at you. "As I said, you're welcome."

You squeeze your fists together. "Now what?"

"Now…" He pokes at the fire with a long stick as the embers catch. "It's pitch black outside—better to stay in the cave overnight. You'll be safe here until the morning—you can have my bed."

He's indicating the pile of leaves in the corner. It's not exactly 1500 thread count satin sheets, but it might be more comfortable than your thin mattress at home.

"When the sun comes up, I'll help you get your car free," he says. "And you can go on your way."

"I appreciate that."

He nods. "My name is Robert, by the way."

"*Robert?*"

He turns away from the fire to glare at you. "What's wrong with the name Robert?"

"Nothing," you say quickly. "I just expected a name that was more… unusual. Like, I don't know… Behemoth or Thundercore or… Chupacabra."

"Chupacabra sucked the blood out of goats," he says.

You did not know that about Chupacabra. Also, why did he say it like Chupacabra is an old buddy of his? Did the two of them go goat-sucking together?

"Anyway," Robert says, "I'm sorry my name isn't more exciting."

"That's all right." You curl up on the ground, tucking your legs underneath your body. "I'm Sloan, by the way."

"Nice to meet you, Sloan."

"Nice to meet you, Robert."

You sit for a moment in companionable silence. Every sound you make in this cave seems to echo around you. You wonder what it must be like living here.

"Do you…" You scan the cave for signs of other similar creatures, but it's just you and him and the hitchhiker. "Do you live here all alone?"

"Yes," he answers, although there's a slight hesitation there.

You arch your eyebrows at him. "Have you always been alone?"

"Not always," he says. "I used to live here with my

wife Nicole, but she… she vanished a few years back."
His gruff voice chokes up with emotion. "I found her
footprints in the snow, but the trail went cold. I searched
everywhere on Peyton's Peak to find her. I spent an
entire year tracking her scent. But I never found her."

"I… I'm so sorry."

He stares down at his hands. "Someone must have
taken her. I don't know who it was, but I can only hope
that one day that person will pay the price."

"I'm sure they will," you say, even though you're
sure of no such thing.

His lips turn down, but then he shakes his head, as if
to clear it. "Are you hungry?"

You hesitate. You're actually starving since you
didn't get dinner before you hit the road, but you're not
sure what sort of food this creature will serve you. What
if he decides to cook the hitchhiker? Of course, you
shouldn't feel so bad about that, given the hitchhiker
was apparently trying to kill you earlier today.

Anyway, you can't go the entire night without eating,
can you?

To accept food from the abominable snowman, turn to
Chapter 29 (page 71)

To turn down his offer of food, turn to Chapter 26
(page 63)

26

You don't know what abominable snowmen eat, and you don't want to know. You would rather go hungry than drink goat blood.

"No, thanks," you say.

"Are you sure?" he asks. "I thought I heard your stomach rumbling earlier."

He's right, but you're not going to admit it. Anyway, you can go a day without eating. People don't need to eat every single day.

The snowman makes food for himself. Truthfully, it doesn't look like anything scary. In fact, it looks like he's eating some cereal. But you've already committed yourself to this decision.

After a little while, you turn in on the bed of leaves in the corner. Unfortunately, your willpower isn't as strong as you thought, because you wake up in the middle of the night, with an empty, gnawing sensation in the pit of your belly.

You've never been so hungry in your entire life.

You get up out of bed, your legs weak from hunger. Robert is asleep in a pile beside the fire, snoring louder than a chainsaw. He doesn't seem aware of anything going on around him.

The hitchhiker isn't nearly as sound a sleeper. He wakes up and makes frantic grunting noises under his gag, but you ignore his attempts to get your attention. However, you notice there's a duffel bag by his side, which he'd been carrying on the road when you passed him by. You wonder if that contains any food.

You eye the duffel bag, your stomach roaring. It isn't right to go through somebody else's belongings, but also, he's already tied up. It seems like the worst has already happened to this guy. Anyway, it's not your fault that he's here. Robert was the one who captured him and tied him up. You're just hungry.

To open the duffel bag, turn to Chapter 27 (page 65)

To go hunting for food elsewhere, turn to Chapter 28 (page 68)

27

THIS DUFFEL BAG IS YOUR BEST CHANCE FOR FOOD. AND it's not like you're going to steal the hitchhiker's belongings. You're just looking for some chips or beef jerky.

You unzip the duffel bag, your stomach growling painfully. The first thing you see is a bunch of clothing. That makes sense, you suppose. You fish around a little more, and you pull out items one by one. A mini sewing kit. A roll of duct tape. A color photograph.

You hold up the photo, and to your surprise, it's a picture of a giraffe. Even stranger, he has crossed out the giraffe with a Sharpie marker. You're not sure what to make of this, but it's not food, so you put it back in the bag.

The next thing you find in the bag is a wooden box that is latched shut. When the hitchhiker sees you remove the box, he starts jerking against his restraints frantically. You ignore him and undo the latch to open it, wondering if the box contains something valuable like jewelry or cash.

It's not jewelry or cash. It's... a bunch of dust.

For a moment, you think the dust could be hot chocolate mix, or something along those lines. But you take a little taste and—no, definitely just dust. You pour it out onto the ground while the hitchhiker moans like you just punched him in the face. He needs to calm the hell down. He has much worse problems than a dirty box being cleaned out. You did him a favor.

Finally, you hit paydirt. You find a baggie of blueberries buried deep in the bag. There are only a handful of berries, but you don't need many. Only enough to calm your empty stomach.

You eat the berries quickly and then return the plastic to the duffel bag. You zip it up, then get to your feet to try to sleep now that you're not so desperately hungry anymore.

You feel better for a short time and almost drift off to sleep, but then, all of a sudden, you are wide awake again. Your mouth is almost painfully dry, and when you try to swallow, it's difficult.

You sit up on the bed of leaves, and find that your heart is pounding and you're covered in a layer of sweat. You try to stand up, but a sharp pain in your abdomen knocks the wind out of you. You feel like you're about to throw up, and you want to get away from the bed to do it, but your legs don't seem to work, so you just turn your head to the side and vomit next to the bed.

You are very dizzy. Could it be from a lack of food? But it hasn't even been 24 hours since you've eaten a full meal. Plus, you ate those berries.

Wait.

The *berries*...

They looked like blueberries, but somehow, they didn't taste like blueberries. They tasted sweet, but also kind of bitter, almost like a tomato, which was very strange. You were so hungry, though—you didn't give it a second thought. After all, why would the hitchhiker have poison berries in his bag?

Another wave of nausea hits you, and you vomit once more. When you raise your eyes, you notice that the hitchhiker is watching you, a smile playing on his lips. He continues watching you as your heart beats wildly, your blood pressure plummets, and finally, you collapse and die from cardiac shock.

THE END

Want to try for a different ending? Turn back to Chapter 1 (page 1)!

28

————

You're very hungry, but you're not going to stoop to the level of going through a stranger's duffel bag, searching for food. There's got to be food around here somewhere.

You take a stick from the ground and ignite the end of it with the embers in the dying fire. That should provide enough light for you to search the cave.

You spend the next hour wandering around, searching for some sort of food, all the while growing hungrier and hungrier. Maybe you shouldn't have expected much in a dark cave in the middle of winter, but you were hoping for something edible *somewhere*.

Just as you're about to give up and go back to sleep, you come across something growing on the ground. It looks like…

A patch of mushrooms.

Granted, you've heard stories about mushrooms sometimes being toxic, but these don't look like poison mushrooms. They look totally normal, like button mushrooms. Besides, at this point, you're too hungry to care. If you hallucinate a little, so what? It might be fun.

You pluck a few of the mushrooms from the ground and eat them raw. They taste fine, like normal mushrooms. Satisfied, you return to your bed and try to get back to sleep, now that your stomach isn't empty.

You feel better for a short time and almost drift back to sleep, but then, all of a sudden, you are wide awake again. Except somehow you're not in a cave anymore. While you were sleeping, you were transported to some sort of wonderland filled with chocolate milk waterfalls and cotton candy trees. You sit up in your bed, which is made from marshmallows!

You dance around the wonderland, stripping off your clothes to enjoy the lovely tropical breeze. It is truly a magical paradise! You even come across Blair's car, which is now made from fudge—you reach out and grab a chunk of it, then pop it in your mouth.

But clearly, the best part is the chocolate waterfall, and you can't possibly go home without jumping off it. You stand at the precipice of the fountain, gazing down at the frothy, warm chocolate below. It looks so inviting. You can't wait to jump in.

"Sloan! Sloan, what are you doing? You're going to fall off the mountain!"

In the distance, you can hear the abominable snowman shouting something to you, but you can't quite make it out. It doesn't matter anyway—he'll only spoil your fun. You hurl yourself off the edge of the waterfall, your legs swinging wildly in the air. And then you are falling…

Falling…
Falling…

THE END

Want to try for a different ending? Turn back to
Chapter 1 (page 1)!

29

You're worried about what kind of food an abominable snowman might serve you, but at this point, you're too hungry to care.

"Don't worry," the abominable snowman says, as if reading your mind. "I won't make you eat anything weird."

"What sort of food do you eat out here?"

"Oh, mostly frosted flakes."

Robert makes you both bowls of frosted flakes, and you sit together on the cold ground, consuming your dinners. You eat with a spoon, but the yeti uses his hands. Still, he is surprisingly graceful. His hands are large and masculine, yet there's something oddly delicate about them, like a piano-player's hands.

"Do you ever get bored out here?" you ask him.

"Not really," he says. "I really like to play hockey, so that eats up some time."

Ooh, he's a hockey player. Hockey players are *so* hot.

You blink, surprised by your own thoughts. Why are

you thinking about the abominable snowman being hot? A couple of hours ago, you were terrified of him. You thought he was going to eat you. And now…

Robert looks up at you. There's something in his gaze that makes you wonder if he's thinking the same thing you are.

"The truth is," he says, "I might not be bored, but I do get lonely here a lot."

"I see," you murmur.

"And," he adds, "it's been nice having you here tonight, Sloan."

"It's been nice being here tonight," you reply, and you're surprised to find that you absolutely mean it. "*Really* nice."

Robert stretches, revealing his taut chest. Under that white fur, his body is covered in bulging muscles. He's the picture of raw masculinity, in yeti form.

Your eyes meet across the fire. The desire in his eyes is unmistakable—he is tacitly letting you know that if you want him, he's yours. But do you want him?

It has, after all, been 19 months since you've had a boyfriend. And you have a feeling that this abominable snowman is a very skilled lover. But at the same time, he's not pressuring you. The choice is in your hands.

To mate with the abominable snowman, turn to Chapter 30 (page 73)

To politely decline his advances, turn to Chapter 31 (page 75)

30

You can't resist this sexy abominable snowman hockey player. Over the next several hours, you end up making sweet love by the fire, and then you fall asleep wrapped in his warm, furry arms.

The next morning, you awaken, feeling well rested and content for the first time in a long time. Robert must have gently disentangled himself from you while you were sleeping, and now he is cooking something on the fire. When he sees you are awake, he flashes you a smile that shows all his fangs.

"Hello, sleepyhead," he says.

You return his smile. "That was nice. *Really* nice."

"It was, wasn't it?" He reaches for your hand, and you give it to him. "I've been so lonely since Nicole disappeared. But you've made me feel whole again." He squeezes your hand. "I hope you'll stay for at least a little while."

You think of the dinner party that you stood up last night, and the money you won't earn to pay your rent.

You have nowhere else to go, but even if you did, there's nowhere else you'd rather be than here with him.

"I'll stay," you tell him.

An amazing aroma fills the cave. Whatever Robert is cooking for breakfast, it smells incredible—like nothing you've ever experienced before. Your mouth starts to water.

"What are you cooking?" you ask.

The yeti jerks his head at the space on the ground where the hitchhiker had been lying last night. Now, all that is left of him is a pile of clothes and his duffel bag.

"I don't *just* eat frosted flakes," Robert explains.

For breakfast, you feast on scrambled eggs with a side of hitchhiker bacon. He is delicious.

THE END

Want to try for a different ending? Turn back to Chapter 1 (page 1)!

31

As attractive as the abominable snowman is, you must decline his advances. He is, after all, not human. Also, you have a life back in the real world, and you need to get back to it.

You spend the rest of the night in the cave. In the morning, the hitchhiker seems to have gone—perhaps Robert set him free. He makes you a delicious scramble with bacon. It's the best bacon you've ever tasted, but you notice a little bit of denim mixed in with your food. You don't comment.

Robert helps you get home, and you can return Blair's car in one piece. Unfortunately, since you missed out on the job at the dinner party, you have to figure out another way to earn some money.

In a fit of inspiration, you write the first chapter of a book. When you show it to Blair, she is so impressed, she decides to let you stay in the room rent-free while you're getting it published.

A year later, your book *That Pucking Snowman* debuts

at number one on the *New York Times* bestseller list, where it stays for the next two years. The movie is coming out next week.

THE END

Want to try for a different ending? Turn back to Chapter 1 (page 1)!

32

YOU DECIDE TO TURN RIGHT AT THE FORK IN THE ROAD. Sharp turns sound scary, but you're worried about how the car will handle in snow. It's safer to stick with the cleared path, even if it has twisty turns. You'll drive slowly.

As promised, the road ahead of you is incredibly narrow and dark. Even with your brights on, you're terrified that you're going to go careening off the side of the mountain and plummet to your death. Despite your lack of money, you're beginning to think that agreeing to this job was a mistake. You should've stayed home and read a book or something.

After driving another half hour with your hands gripping the steering wheel so tightly that your fingers have turned white, you reach an imposing iron gate with a large W emblazoned on it. You check Avery's directions to confirm—yes, this is it.

The sky is cloudy, only partially illuminated by a full moon. You keep your headlights on for visibility as you drive closer to the gate, finally coming to a halt right in front of it. It doesn't automatically swing open, but you spot an intercom mounted to the right of the gate. You put the car in park, leaving the engine running, and walk over to the intercom.

The intercom is a small metal device with a speaker and a single button. You press the button, and there's a burst of static loud enough that you take a step back. This isn't too promising.

"Hello?" you say into the intercom. "This is Sloan?" You're not sure why that comes out as a question, but somehow it does. "I'm here for the waitressing job?"

No reply. Only another loud burst of static. You try to push the gates open manually, but they don't budge.

But then, after several beats, the iron gates begin to part. They move as if in slow motion, the hinges screaming in protest.

There's something about this estate that is really sketchy. True, you have driven two hours to get here, but you're beginning to worry that there's more to this waitressing job than meets the eye. And maybe you should get out of here while you still can.

But you realize once you go through these gates, you have to go through with it. This is your final chance to turn back.

To turn around and go home, turn to Chapter 6 (page 14)

To proceed to the house, turn to Chapter 33 (page 79)

33

YOU'VE DRIVEN TWO HOURS TO GET HERE, SO IT WOULD be ridiculous to turn back at this point. Besides, you really need the money. Going home isn't an option.

So you get back in your car and drive through the iron gates.

They slam shut behind you with a sickening clang. It's clear that you're not going anywhere for the rest of the night. The gates are locked behind you.

The driveway to the front of the house is long and winding, but on the plus side, at least there's no danger of falling off the mountain. You follow the path until you reach the large mansion. To the right of the house, there's a paved area where about a dozen cars are parked—it seems that there's quite the crowd at the dinner party tonight. You pull over beside the other cars.

You step out into the cold night air, shivering at a gust of wind that goes right through your coat. You hug your chest as you hurry in the direction of the front door. When you get there, you press the doorbell, which chimes loudly enough that you take a step back, startled.

A second later, the door to the house swings open.

A man is standing before you. He's wearing a white dress shirt and white tie, paired with a black tailcoat and dress pants. He's about your age, maybe in his early 20s, and he is startlingly handsome. He has thick hair that's so blond, it's nearly white, clear gray eyes, a hint of a cleft in his chin, and cheekbones to die for. You could stare at this man all night long. (All morning too…)

Whoa. Is *this* who you're working for tonight? Avery should have led with this information. *By the way, Sloan, your boss is a legit fox.*

"Hello," the man says in a deep voice that is, if possible, even more gorgeous than he looks.

"Hi," you say in a squeaky voice that is not at all gorgeous. "I'm Sloan."

"My name is Carson," the man says. "I'm the butler for the Wentworth family. Won't you come this way?"

Oh, he's the *butler*. You suppose that makes more sense. Actually, that's a good thing. Nobody who actually *lives* in this house would hook up with the likes of you. But you have a real shot with the butler.

Not that you should be thinking about such things. You're here to do your job, earn your rent money, and get the hell out of here.

Although if there's some downtime and Carson wants to make out with you, you wouldn't have any objections.

Carson leads you into the house. You can hear

Avery's voice coming from another room, getting louder by the second. She'll be here any moment now.

"Hey." Carson's voice is suddenly urgent as he grabs your arm, his gaze darting around the room. At first, you think he might want to kiss you, but instead, he leans in and hisses in your ear, "*You are in danger.*"

Turn to Chapter 34 (page 82)

34

YOU ARE IN DANGER.

Carson's words are ringing in your ears as Avery dashes out, wearing a black dress and white apron that matches Carson's attire, her red hair pinned back from her face. When she sees you, she throws her arms around you like you haven't seen each other in years.

"Sloan!" she cries. "I'm *so* glad you could make it! I don't know what we would've done if you hadn't come!"

That seems extreme. They simply would have had to make do with one waitress. It's not like the entire party is hanging on your presence. Avery can be *so* dramatic.

"It was a rough drive," you say, "but I'm here."

Avery links her arm into yours. "Let me introduce you to the hosts and some of the guests. They will be thrilled to meet you."

They will? It's been your experience that most people aren't that excited to meet the wait staff at a party, but some rich people are very eccentric.

Carson is just standing there, his back straight, his

face expressionless. *You are in danger.* Did he really say that to you? It feels almost as if you might have imagined the whole thing. You certainly don't feel like you're in any danger. This is just a party for a bunch of old rich people—what danger could you possibly be in?

"What sort of party is this, anyway?" you ask Avery as she drags you into another room.

"It's a dinner club," she explains. "They call themselves the Adventurous Eaters Club. They eat all sorts of exotic animals, apparently."

"Exotic animals? Like what?"

"Oh, you know." She shrugs. "Like ostrich or something."

Avery leads you into a room where about a dozen people are sipping on glasses of wine and chatting together. The room reeks of Old Money, from the expensive suits to the designer gowns to the jewelry and Rolex watches. The men all have gray or white hair, and the women all look like they've had Botox. But they do, indeed, look very pleased to see you when you enter the room.

"Hello!" This enthusiastic greeting comes from a gray-haired man wearing a sleek gray suit that contrasts sharply with his gentle smile. "This must be our new waitress, Sloan."

"It sure is," Avery answers for you.

The man looks pleased by her answer. "It's so good to meet you, Sloan. My name is Davenport Wentworth, and I'm the host of this dinner party."

"It's nice to meet you, Mr. Wentworth," you say politely.

Mr. Wentworth takes your extended hand, but instead of shaking it, he lifts it to his lips and kisses the back of your hand. But it wasn't a kiss—not exactly. Maybe it's your imagination, but it almost seems like he *licked* you. That's ridiculous, though.

Mr. Wentworth insists on introducing you to all the guests in the room by name, even though you immediately forget all of their names. Hopefully, you won't be called upon to remember them later.

"Sloan," Mr. Wentworth says, as he introduces you to a tall, gangly man with large spectacles perched on his nose. "This is my dear friend, Heinrich van Houten."

"Ah, Sloan," he says in a thick Eastern European accent as he clasps your hand in both of his. "I cannot wait for you to be served to us."

Mr. Wentworth shoots him a look. "Sloan, please excuse Heinrich's English. What he means is, he can't wait for you *to serve us*. Our dinners, that is. We're famished!"

"Oh, yes, of course," Heinrich corrects himself. "*To serve us*. My mistake."

Okay...

"Is dinner almost ready?" you ask.

"Dinner is... in progress," Mr. Wentworth says. "The chef does not wish to prepare it until soon before we are ready to eat. He wishes everything to be... fresh."

"Do you need me to change into a uniform?"

"No, no." Mr. Wentworth smiles at you. "There's no need for you to change."

"Sounds good," you say, glad to be allowed to remain in your own clothes. "Do you want to show me the kitchen now?"

"Yes, of course. But first…" He reaches into his jacket pocket and pulls out a camera. "I need to get your photo for your ID badge."

ID badge? That seems a little like overkill for a one-night gig. Especially after Carson's cryptic warning, the idea makes you uncomfortable.

But then again, what's the harm in having your photo taken?

To agree to the photo, turn to Chapter 35 (page 86)

To refuse the photo, turn to Chapter 36 (page 88)

35

IT DEFINITELY MAKES YOU UNCOMFORTABLE TO HAVE your photo taken, but on the other hand, aren't all rich people eccentric? What's the harm?

"Sure," you agree.

"Excellent." Mr. Wentworth gestures across the room. "Could you please stand in front of that wall over there?"

You obediently stand in front of a white wall. Mr. Wentworth pulls a camera out of his coat pocket while everyone in the room watches with interest, especially Heinrich.

"Very good," Mr. Wentworth says, "but you're a little too low. Would you mind getting on that step so you'll be higher up?"

You look down at where he's pointing. It takes you a moment to figure out what he wants you to stand on.

"That's a scale!" you protest.

"Is it?" he replies vaguely. "Well, no mind. Just step

on it for a moment so you'll be a little taller, and I can take your photo."

This is extremely bizarre, but you're not about to quit after spending two hours driving here. You step on the scale, hoping this whole ordeal will be over soon.

"She is 124 point six pounds!" Heinrich announces.

"*Excuse* me?" you start to say, but then Mr. Wentworth snaps your photo, and it's all over.

Mr. Wentworth looks down at the digital display on the camera, smiling to himself. "Wonderful picture. We'll get this printed right away."

"Um, great," you say.

"Now," he says, "let me show you our dining room."

Turn to Chapter 37 (page 90)

36

"I'm sorry," you say. "I don't feel comfortable having my photo taken for an ID card. I hope you understand."

"That is very disappointing," Mr. Wentworth says. "We always get photos."

"But I'm only here for the night. Why do I need an ID card?"

"Sloan." Avery pinches your arm. "Stop being such a drama queen. Just let them take your photo."

At this point, it feels like you might have made a big deal over nothing, and it would be better just to give in. But you've made the decision not to allow your photo to be taken, and you intend to stick to it.

"Do not worry," Heinrich van Houten says to Mr. Wentworth in a low voice. "Her photos are all over the social media."

Well, that's true. But what does that have to do with an ID badge?

"All right," Mr. Wentworth sighs. "I'm disappointed,

but if you don't want me to take your photo, we won't do it."

"Thank you. I appreciate that."

"Now," he says, "let me show you our dining room."

Turn to Chapter 37 (page 90)

37

Mr. Wentworth leads you down a long hallway to what turns out to be the largest dining room you have ever seen. It looks like something out of the Gilded Age, from the antique chairs and dining table to the grand chandelier dangling from the ceiling.

"This," he says, "is where we will be dining tonight."

You can't help but notice the framed photos mounted on the walls. It takes you a moment to realize that the photos are all of various animals. But most of them are not animals you've ever seen before. You struggle to recognize even one of them.

"These are some of the animals sampled in the past by the Adventurous Eaters Club," Mr. Wentworth tells you proudly. We always get a picture of them for the wall before their sacrifice."

"I see…"

"That's a spotted genet." Mr. Wentworth points to a picture of something that looks like a cross between a raccoon and a leopard. "And that over there is a Cuvier's dwarf crocodile." He smiles fondly. "It took forever to get that little devil tender enough to eat."

Your gaze lingers on a photo of a creature that looks a little bit like an ape, but with white fur. You've never seen anything like it before. "What is that?"

"I'm so glad you asked, Sloan." He is now practically beaming. "That is an abominable snowman."

"An… abominable snowman?"

"That's right."

Apparently, they are serving imaginary animals at their dinner club. "The abominable snowman isn't real."

"Oh, it is very much real," Mr. Wentworth assures you. "She's real, and she put up one hell of a fight. But in the end, we got her. And she was quite delicious."

You're not sure what to say to that, so instead you ask, "What are you serving tonight?"

"Oh," he says, "I'll let that be a surprise."

Surprise? Well, whatever it is, maybe you can sample a tiny bit. This will probably be your only chance to taste a dragon or Godzilla or whatever the hell it is they're making in there. Although you love animals and hate the idea of them being kept in cages, you also respect the food chain and are not a vegetarian.

"Now…" He rubs his hands together eagerly. "We still have a little time before dinner. Would you care for a tour of the house? Or would you like to go straight to the kitchen?"

To take a tour of the house, turn to Chapter 38
(page 93)

To go straight to the kitchen, turn to Chapter 46
(page 111)

38

THERE'S NO POINT IN SITTING AROUND THE KITCHEN doing nothing, so you decide to take the tour. You've never been inside a huge mansion like this before, and you bet it's pretty cool.

"Thank you," you say. "A tour would be wonderful."

"Splendid!" Mr. Wentworth exclaims. "A little walking will help me work up my appetite for our magnificent feast tonight."

You follow Mr. Wentworth up a large staircase with a banister wider than your thighs. It almost feels like somebody is watching you, and when you turn around, you notice that Carson is standing at the foot of the stairs. He is following you with his eyes, a deep crease between his pale brows.

You are in danger.

Your neck tickles slightly at the memory of his hot breath whispering in your ear. He seemed so worried, but you're still not sure why. Mr. Wentworth seems eccentric, sure, but definitely not dangerous.

Maybe it was a pickup line. Sort of like taking a girl to a scary movie.

The flight of stairs feels almost endless, and when you get to the top, you are out of breath. Mr. Wentworth, on the other hand, is not the slightest bit winded. He is at least forty years older than you, but he seems to have boundless energy. Without so much as a pause, he leads you to a closed door at the very end of the hall. He pauses with his hand on the knob. "This," he says dramatically, "is our home theater!"

He throws open the door. You're not sure what you expected—possibly a large movie screen and rows of stadium seats, a popcorn machine. Instead, there is just a video camera on a tripod, which is pointed at a twin bed covered only in a stained sheet.

"Um, very nice," you say.

"We get a *lot* of use out of it," he assures you. "Especially on Super Bowl Sunday."

"I'm sure…"

The next stop on your tour is a room he refers to as the "library." Again, you expected rows of bookcases, but instead, there is only one single stack of books piled up to the high ceiling, teetering on the brink of collapse.

"This is your library?" you say in disbelief.

"Gorgeous, isn't it?"

"Um." You peer at the stack of books. "If you want to read one of them, how do you get it out of the stack?"

"Exactly!" he says, as if that answered your question.

He closes the door to the library, and you continue to the next door. "This," he tells you, his voice thrumming with excitement, "is our Olympic-sized swimming pool."

He opens the door, and while the space is certainly large enough for an Olympic-sized swimming pool, the only water in the room is a small puddle in the center of the room. But Mr. Wentworth looks so proud of the display that you feel compelled to say, "Wow."

"Ah," he says, "if you're impressed now, wait until you see the top floor."

He leads you to the very end of the hallway, to another set of stairs, this one a lot more narrow. The lights are not as bright here, and you start to feel a little claustrophobic. You're not sure if you should continue up to the top floor. And once again, Carson's words echo in your head.

You are in danger.

Maybe it would be best to end the tour here. Mr. Wentworth will surely understand.

To ask to go back to the kitchen, turn to Chapter 39 (page 96)

To continue up to the top floor, turn to Chapter 40 (page 97)

39

"MR. WENTWORTH," YOU SAY, "I THINK IT WOULD BE best if we cut our tour short here."

He frowns, his eyes hardening. "Why? Aren't you enjoying yourself? Not many people get to see inside this estate. You're enjoying a rare privilege."

"Yes," you acknowledge, "but I came here to work, and I'd feel better if I got the lay of the land in the kitchen first."

Mr. Wentworth is quiet for a moment, a shadow crossing over his features. Your stomach fills with butterflies, and you worry that you've angered him. But then, his face lights up.

"I admire your work ethic, Sloan," he says. "Come on. Let's head down to the kitchen."

Turn to Chapter 46 (page 111)

40

Even though something in your gut is telling you it's a mistake, you follow Mr. Wentworth up to the top floor. This staircase is just as long as the other one, and about five times on your way up, you consider telling him you want to turn around and go back. But at this point, you're committed. You've made the decision.

When you finally get to the top of the stairs, there are two closed doors before you. Mr. Wentworth leads you to the first of the two doors.

"This," Mr. Wentworth says, his hand on the knob, "is our deluxe guest room."

He throws open the door like he's leading you into a grand banquet hall. So you're a little surprised to find that the only things inside the room are a small cot covered in dark red stains, a mini fridge, and a bucket.

"Um, do you get a lot of guests?" you ask.

"Oh, loads," he says. "They say it's like staying at a mini spa."

It doesn't look like a mini spa to you, although it is,

admittedly, a little nicer than your own bedroom at home.

He closes the door to that room behind him, and then you proceed to the final room. Mr. Wentworth is now positively beaming.

"This is my favorite part of the tour," he tells you. "Prepare yourself."

Then he opens the door. And you have to admit, you're pretty surprised by what you see before you.

The room is filled with animal cages.

There are at least half a dozen cages, but only one of them contains an actual animal. It's some sort of wolf-like creature with a heavy build, white fur, and razor-sharp fangs. It deeply pains you to see any animal locked in a cell, so your heart goes out to this poor wolf. You can't even imagine how awful it must be to be locked in that tiny cage in a rich guy's attic. Plus—let's face it—Mr. Wentworth is probably going to eat the creature.

"This," Mr. Wentworth informs you, "is a dire wolf." He gazes at the animal with reverence, and possibly some hunger. "Isn't she *spectacular*?"

"A dire wolf?" you repeat. "Aren't they extinct?"

"Oh, no," he laughs. "My dear, you need to brush up on your history."

Mr. Wentworth opens his mouth as if he's about to give you a little impromptu lecture about the dire wolf, which you are almost 100% sure is extinct, but before he can, a male voice calls up the stairs.

"Mr. Wentworth." Carson materializes at the top of the stairwell, his expression grave. "Your immediate attention is required in the kitchen. The oven is having a malfunction."

"Oh dear." Mr. Wentworth shakes his head, distressed. "I'll be right down."

Carson waits for Mr. Wentworth to start down the steps, and then he follows behind him. But before he disappears, Carson casts one last look over his shoulder at you. The warning in his gray eyes is unmistakable.

Once the two of them are gone, you are left alone in the attic. Well, just you and the dire wolf.

That poor wolf! She looks so sad in her cage. No animal should be trapped in a cage. It's *wrong*. Just looking at her is physically painful for you.

That's when you notice a key hanging from a hook mounted on the wall of the room.

You suspect the key must open the cage. After all, what other purpose could it possibly serve? If you want, you could set the wolf free. Nobody could stop you.

But maybe that's not such a good idea. After all, the wolf has very sharp teeth. And she looks hungry.

What should you do?

To open the cage, turn to Chapter 41 (page 100)

To leave the carnivorous animal with sharp fangs secure in her cage, turn to Chapter 42 (page 102)

41

Yes, the wolf looks dangerous and hungry. But she is a living creature, and you cannot leave her trapped in a cage. You couldn't live with yourself if you did that, especially when you have a chance to set her free.

Besides, the wolf won't hurt you. She will surely understand that you're on her side. Animals sense things like that.

You grab the key off the wall. Slowly, you approach the cage, key in hand. You allow her to sniff your hand, so she'll get used to the scent of you, but she lets out a growl, and you pull your hand away before she bites it off.

"Hey, girl," you say, "I'm going to let you out of there."

The wolf lets out another growl, and a glob of saliva drips from her lips. You're not entirely sure how to interpret that, and you don't try too hard.

You fit the key into the lock with hands that are only

slightly shaking. For a moment, it doesn't turn, and you think that all this buildup was for nothing, but then you apply a little more force, and you hear a click.

Slowly, you pull open the cage door. You take a step back, bracing yourself for the wolf to leap up and rip you limb from limb. But to your surprise, the wolf does not claw you limb from limb. In fact, she doesn't move at all.

"Go!" you hiss at the animal. "You're free! Get out of here before they eat you!"

But the wolf does not budge.

Stupid wolf.

Well, that was all for nothing. As the saying goes, you can open a wolf's cage, but you can't make her leap out and rip out the throats of everyone in the house.

Sighing, you leave the room and head back downstairs.

Turn to Chapter 42 (page 102)

42

WHEN YOU GET BACK DOWNSTAIRS, AVERY IS WAITING
for you. She flashes you a smile that shows all of her
teeth. You've known Avery a long time, but you've never
seen her so thrilled to see you.

"Mr. Wentworth told me to send you into the
kitchen," she says. "There was an issue with the stove,
but it seems to be resolved."

"Sure," you say. "Will you show me where it is?"

"Actually," Avery says, "I have to set the table. But
it's right down the hallway on your left. You can't
miss it."

She seems so confident you'll be able to find the
kitchen, but this place is huge. Still, you're sure that if
you get lost, someone will point you in the right direction. "Okay, no problem."

Avery disappears down the hall to the dining room.
You're about to follow her directions to your own destination when the doorbell rings, echoing through the
entire house.

You freeze, waiting for Carson to materialize and answer the door. He's the butler, so presumably, he should be the one doing any door-answering. But he is nowhere in sight.

You're not sure what to do. Nobody listed answering the door as one of your responsibilities, and you don't want to overstep. But if you're standing right here and the doorbell is ringing, it seems ridiculous not to answer it. You don't want to be reprimanded for not doing a good job tonight. What if they dock your pay?

Then again, that's what the butler is for. You don't want to get in trouble for not greeting a guest properly. Ugh, what are you supposed to do?

To answer the door, turn to Chapter 43 (page 104)

To continue to the kitchen, turn to Chapter 46 (page 111)

43

You decide you'd better open the door. It's just good manners, after all. Especially since it's cold out, and you don't want to leave a visitor waiting at the doorstep.

You notice, however, that there is a chain lock on the door. That means you can unlock it and see who is out there without opening it all the way. You suppose that with a large mansion like this, you can't be too careful, although the gate around the estate seemed like a fortress.

You unlock the door, and when you peek out through the crack, you are stunned. Standing before you is the hitchhiker that you passed way back on the road. You recognize his big bushy beard and unkempt hair.

"Oh, thank God," he cries. "I've been wandering this mountain for the last hour. It's so cold out there. I thought I was going to freeze to death!"

"That sounds awful," you say.

The hitchhiker hugs his chest for warmth, bouncing

on his heels. "Could you let me in? Just for a minute? I won't bother you. I just need to call a friend to pick me up."

It's a reasonable request. The man wants shelter on a cold night, just for the length of a phone call. Except...

"Um," you say, "I'm not sure if I should. This isn't my house..."

"I understand," he says, "but I'm not looking for a place to stay. Just the use of your phone. *Please.*"

You start to reach into your pocket to give him your cell phone, but then you remember there's no service out here. The only way he'll be able to use the phone is to come inside and use the landline.

"*Please.*" His teeth chatter against each other. "It's *so* cold out here. I just need to call my friend."

"Uh..."

His eyes widen. "*Please.* If you don't let me inside, I'm going to *die* out here."

Obviously, you don't want this man to *die*. But you also don't know if it's a good idea to let someone you don't know into the house. That's Stranger Danger 101.

What should you do?

To let the hitchhiker inside, turn to Chapter 44 (page 106)

To send the hitchhiker away, turn to Chapter 45 (page 110)

44

YOU CAN'T LET THIS MAN FREEZE TO DEATH OUTSIDE. As a compassionate fellow human, you have to let him in to use the phone.

"Of course," you tell him. "Just let me undo this chain."

"Oh, bless you!" the hitchhiker cries. "You won't regret this."

You close the door, undo the chain, and then throw the door back open. As the door swings open wide, the hitchhiker has a huge smile on his face, which makes you really glad you decided to help him.

"Thank you *so* much," he says.

"You're welc—" you start to say, but your words are cut off when the hitchhiker wraps his fingers around your throat.

He's trying to kill you! The man you took pity on and let inside so he wouldn't freeze is now trying to choke you to death. God, you can't do anything right!

He tightens his grip on your neck. You see spots, and

then everything starts to go dark. He's going to kill you. He's going to—

Moments before you black out, you hear a loud thud from over your head. All at once, the pressure on your neck eases up. You collapse to the floor, gasping for air.

It takes a few seconds for your vision to clear. But when it does, you see Avery standing in front of you, holding a heavy metal tray. The hitchhiker is lying unconscious on the floor.

"What was *that* all about?" Avery asks.

"I let him in to use the phone," you manage. "And then… he tried to… to choke me."

Avery shakes her head. "Sloan, you are far too nice for your own good. Look where it gets you!"

You rub your throat with your hand. You're going to have bruises tomorrow. "We should probably call the police."

Avery looks down at the unconscious man on the floor. She rubs her chin thoughtfully. "Let me get Mr. Wentworth. It's his house, so we should manage it the way he wants us to."

You're not sure exactly what that means. A man just tried to strangle you. It seems like calling the police is a no-brainer.

But before you can protest, Avery has gone off to fetch Mr. Wentworth. He returns right away, an anxious expression on his face. When he sees the hitchhiker on the floor, his eyes widen.

"Well," he says, "this is certainly an interesting turn of events."

"We need to call the police," you say stubbornly.

"Of course we do," he assures you. "And we will. But while I'm dealing with the police, perhaps the two of you could go to the dining room to set the table. No sense in letting this little mishap spoil our evening. The Adventurous Eaters Club has been meeting every year for the last 20 years, and we certainly don't want to miss our yearly meeting because of this intruder."

"I guess so," you agree reluctantly.

You allow Avery to lead you down the hall to the dining room, where the two of you set the table. You don't hear the police arrive, but the next time you return to the foyer, the hitchhiker is gone.

"Avery," you say when you join her in the kitchen. "What happened with that hitchhiker? Did the police come and get him?"

Avery is busy wiping down the kitchen counter. "Oh. Yes, they came and took him off to jail. He won't be bothering you ever again."

"Well, that's a relief."

It's only then that you notice that the pattern on the rag Avery is using to wipe the counter is identical to the one on the hitchhiker's shirt. That's an interesting coincidence.

After the whole mess with the hitchhiker, it actually ends up being a lovely evening. The chef takes forever to finish dinner, and you don't serve the food till nearly midnight, but whatever it is ends up being a big hit, and they reward you with a generous paycheck for your time. After the guests have eaten, you and Avery get a taste, and it's one of the most delicious meals you've ever had.

THE END

Want to try for a different ending? Turn back to
Chapter 1 (page 1)!

45

"I'M SORRY," YOU TELL THE HITCHHIKER. "I'M NOT allowed to let anyone into the house without permission. Could you use another phone?"

"There is no other phone!" the hitchhiker yells. "I need to get inside! Let me in!"

"I'm sorry, but—"

"Let me in!" he hollers. "Please! If you don't let me in, I'm going to die! And it will be on your conscience!"

Oh my.

Pushing away a surge of guilt, you close the door and lock it firmly. He rings the doorbell again, pushing his finger against it so that it sounds like one continuous ring, but you're not going to let him in. Carson is the butler, and he can take care of this situation. Besides, you've got to get to the kitchen.

Turn to Chapter 46 (page 111)

46

THE KITCHEN IS THE LARGEST ONE YOU'VE EVER SEEN. IT has every modern appliance you can imagine, but the most incredible thing is the oven, which seems to take up half the room. It's practically large enough to fit an elephant.

You hope they haven't eaten any elephants. That would be awful. Much worse than the abominable snowman.

"This is one of the most well-equipped non-professional kitchens in the country," Mr. Wentworth tells you proudly. He seems so excited to show you everything. You would think you were the guest of honor here rather than a waitress. "And of course, I'd like you to meet our chef, Jacques. He's one of the greatest chefs in the entire world!"

The chef is a small, dapper man with a pristine white chef jacket and white chef hat. His most remarkable feature is the little mustache on his upper lip that curls at the edges. He beams at you, and as Mr. Wentworth did, he kisses your hand. "It is a true pleasure to meet you, Sloan."

"Likewise," you say.

"Now let me give you a tour of our appliances," Mr. Wentworth says.

He shows you the high-tech "smart" fridge, which has an internal camera, WiFi, and apparently even alerts you when foods are on the brink of expiration. The dishwasher also uses advanced technology that "softens water." You had no idea that water being too hard was such a big issue.

"And this is our top-of-the-line oven." Mr. Wentworth pauses in front of the gigantic oven, which has more buttons on it than a laptop. "It can cook food in convection mode and *super* convection mode."

"Wow," you say, not really sure what either of those words means.

"It also senses how long the food requires cooking," he explains. "If you were to step inside, it would know exactly how long to cook you until you were nice and crispy."

"Um. Amazing."

He seems a bit disappointed that you're not more enthusiastic, but he quickly moves on. "Now let me show you our serving utensils."

You follow him to a counter that contains a stack of metal trays, utensils, serving spoons, and wine glasses. Each item gleams in the overhead lights.

"The food will go on the serving tray," he says, "and you will bring it out to the dining room."

Seems straightforward enough. "No problem."

You pick up one of the serving trays, which is heavier than you thought it would be. It must be very expensive and well made. It has been scrubbed and polished to the point where you can see your reflection on the surface. And when you tilt the tray slightly, you can see the reflection of the chef behind you.

Hmm. That's strange.

In Jacques's reflection in the metal tray, he appears to be hovering behind you, holding what appears to be a butcher knife. The expression on his face is decidedly menacing.

Your heart speeds up. What's going on here? It's not possible that this dapper little chef means you harm, is it?

Your grip tightens on the metal tray. If Jacques does intend to hurt you, you have a way to defend yourself and save your life.

On the other hand, if you smack the chef on the head with this tray and knock him out, you could kiss this job goodbye.

If you want to hit Jacques on the head with the tray, turn to Chapter 48 (page 116)

If you don't think this is suspicious at all, turn to Chapter 47 (page 114)

47

There's no way Jacques is going to hurt you. He's a chef, not a hired assassin. He's obviously just walking around the kitchen with his chef's knife, as chefs do.

You put down the tray and turn around.

Jacques is startlingly close—much closer than he appeared in the tray. There should be a warning that says "objects in the tray are closer than they appear." If there had been, you would not have been so shocked to find Jacques inches away from you, brandishing a butcher knife.

"Hello again, Sloan," he says.

Although what he really means is "goodbye," because at that moment, he slashes the blade of the butcher knife against your throat.

You collapse to the floor, clutching your neck and gasping for air. You know it's a lost cause, though. You've seen many movies where people have had their throats cut, and none of them ever live. You are going to die.

And the last words you hear before you lose consciousness are, "Don't you think she'd go well with a nice béarnaise sauce?"

THE END

Want to try for a different ending? Turn back to Chapter 1 (page 1)!

48

THAT CHEF BRANDISHING A KNIFE BEHIND YOU IS TOTALLY suspicious. You don't know exactly why he wants to hurt you, but it's very clear what his intentions are. And you're not going to let him get away with it.

You whirl around, holding the metal tray over your head. When Jacques sees what you're doing, his eyes widen in surprise, and he doesn't have time to react before you bring the tray crashing down on his scalp. He falls to the floor, unconscious. The butcher knife clatters from his hand.

"Hey!" Mr. Wentworth cries. "What do you think you're doing?"

To your horror, it looks like he is fumbling for a knife of his own on the kitchen counter. You don't have time to waste—you've got to get out of here. No job is worth getting your throat slashed by a bunch of psychopaths. God knows what they were thinking.

You hurry out of the kitchen, but you must cut through the dining room in order to get out. Avery has already set the table, and despite everything, you have to admit that the effect is magical. The fine china and silverware gleam under the light of the chandelier. It looks like it will be a lovely dinner—too bad you won't be around to see it.

Just as you're trying to figure out the best way out of here, you notice that a brand new picture has been hung on the wall of the dining room. There's no time to admire the artwork, but somehow your eyes are drawn to this photo of whatever will be served for their meal tonight. You lock in on the image, moving closer to get a better look. It takes a moment for your brain to comprehend the subject of this new photograph.

It's *you*.

Turn to Chapter 49 (page 118)

49

OH GOD. *YOU* WERE FOR DINNER TONIGHT. THE CHEF was going to kill you, and then cook you, and serve you to all those rich people. And the oven was going to know exactly how long to cook you to get you nice and crispy.

Carson was right. You *are* in danger.

You've got to get out of here. You've got to make a run for your car and get as far away from here as you possibly can.

You stumble out of the dining room, not sure exactly where you're going, but just knowing that you have to get the hell out of here—*now*. As soon as you get back into the hallway, you run smack into Avery. Oh, thank God.

"Avery!" You grab her more roughly than you intended. "We've got to get out of here! Right now!"

Avery's eyes widen. "Why? What's wrong?"

"These people are out of their minds!" you cry. "The chef in the kitchen tried to kill me! I think… This sounds insane, but I think they were going to *eat* me."

"*Eat* you?" Avery gasps. "Sloan, are you sure about that?"

"Yes!" A sob bursts from your throat. "I've got to get out of here right now. Which way is the exit?"

"The exit?"

"Yes, the exit! I need to get out of here!"

"Right, right…" Avery looks around, rubbing her chin. "Actually, if you really need to get out of here, and you don't want anyone to see you, there's a secret exit through the back. That's probably the safest way if you really think that you're, you know, in danger."

"Great! What are you waiting for? Let's go!"

"Well, okay. Let me just get my—"

"Avery, we need to go!"

"Right." She nods, as if to herself. "Let's go."

Avery leads you down a hallway, and you follow close behind. As long as the two of you are together, you feel at least somewhat safe. And pretty soon, you'll be out of this awful place.

As you walk down the hall, you pass by some sort of parlor, where the group of would-be diners seems to be congregated. They're standing around, laughing, talking, and drinking wine. Probably working up an appetite.

The fear in your chest is suddenly replaced by fury. These people were going to *eat* you! How *dare* they! You'd really like to give them a piece of your mind.

Is that safe, though? Yes, they are all pretty old. But at the same time, there are a lot more of them than there are of you. If it came down to it, they might be able to overpower you. Even with Avery by your side.

Still, you're itching to go in there and let them know that you are in on their secret, and that they're going to have to hit the McDonald's drive-thru for a Big Mac if they're really that hungry for meat.

If you want to confront the cannibals, turn to Chapter 50 (page 121)

If you want to continue trying to escape, turn to Chapter 58 (page 146)

50

WHO CARES IF YOUR LIFE MIGHT STILL BE IN DANGER? You're not about to walk out of here without telling these boomers that trying to eat you was *totally* uncool.

"Hey." Avery frowns when you stop by the parlor. "What are you doing? I thought you wanted to get out of here…?"

"I do," you say. "But there's one thing I need to do first."

You ignore Avery's protests and march into the parlor. All at once, every set of eyes swivels in your direction. Good, you have their attention.

"Listen to me, people," you say. "I know what you all were trying to do. I know you planned to eat me." You wait for them to deny it. They don't. "And I just want you to let you know how incredibly shitty that was."

You're not sure exactly what sort of response you were expecting. An apology perhaps? *Sorry, we did indeed want to eat you, but we see now that was wrong.* But nobody is saying anything. You could hear a pin drop.

"I mean," you go on, "how would you feel if I ate *you*? I bet you wouldn't like it very much!"

"Of course you would not eat us!" Heinrich finally speaks up in that thick accent. "You could never afford the delicacy of human flesh! Besides," he adds, "all of us would be missed, and you would not."

Ouch. It's true, but still—a low blow.

You realize for the first time that you might have made a mistake stopping at this room. You have under-estimated these old people, who actually seem quite spry all of a sudden. And now they're descending on you, several of them licking their lips. Also, you didn't think they could hurt you, but it turns out they all have weapons—not just weapons, but old-timey weapons. One of them has a trident. Another is holding a spear. Another is holding a stick that has a ball attached to it with little spikes coming out of it. (That probably has a name, but you don't know what it is.)

Oh no. You should have run for it while you still could.

Turn to Chapter 51 (page 123)

51

———

You turn around, hoping to make a run for it, but you realize the door to the room is now closed. You grab the doorknob, but it doesn't turn. Worse, Avery has disappeared.

Did Avery lock you in here?

The old people are descending on you. At any moment, they are going to bludgeon you with their ancient weapons, and then eat you with fava beans and a nice Chianti. It's all over. If only you hadn't stopped in this room, you could have gotten away, but you just *had* to confront them. Now you are completely screwed.

This is it. They're going to kill you. Any second now…

You squeeze your eyes shut, bracing yourself for the impact of the first weapon. But before you can feel anything, a terrifying growl echoes through the room. Your eyes fly open just in time to see the large animal breaking through the lock, bursting the door wide open.

It's a *wolf.*

You can hardly believe your eyes. A *wolf* is in the middle of the room. It's larger than an average wolf, covered in white fur and foaming angrily at the mouth. It lets out a growl that makes all those old people take a step back.

This wolf is *seriously* pissed off at all the old people in this room. The first thing it does is lunge at Heinrich's throat, streaking dark red blood all over its fur. After efficiently disposing of him, the wolf proceeds to the next victim.

You should probably make a run for it, but you are absolutely paralyzed by the scene unfolding in front of you. The wolf is making short work of everyone in this room, ripping through clothing, tearing off arms and legs, shrugging off their attempts to fight against him. You've never seen anything like it. It's like the wolf has superhuman strength. (Superwolf strength?)

And then—*finally*—the last guest has been ripped to shreds by the wolf. Its formerly white coat is now drenched with crimson. Its chest heaves with the exertion of killing everyone in this room—well, everyone except you.

The wolf swivels its gaze to look at you, zeroing in as it stands between you and the door. If you try to run for it, you're pretty sure the wolf will catch you and kill you. Maybe if you just stay very still and look nonthreatening, the wolf won't attack. Isn't their vision based on movement? Or is that only dinosaurs?

To make a run for it, turn to Chapter 52 (page 126)

To stay still, turn to Chapter 53 (page 128)

52

You have to try to run for it. It's your only chance.

The door is hanging open on its hinges. Without a second glance at the wolf, you run as fast as you can in the direction of the door. You don't stop to look behind you.

It's no surprise when the wolf comes out after you. You move as quickly as you can, nearly tripping on a bloody body in the hallway. It only vaguely occurs to you that the body belongs to Avery, who is now just as dead as everyone in that room. You don't even have a chance to mourn your friend, because you need to keep moving. You hurry down the hallway, desperately searching for the way out.

Except when you hazard a look over your shoulder, you don't see anything. You slow to a halt, looking all around you, but somehow, the wolf has vanished into thin air.

Turn to Chapter 54 (page 130)

53

THE WOLF DESCENDS ON YOU, BLOOD AND SALIVA dripping from its lips. It lets out a low growl, and you brace yourself, waiting for the animal to pounce and rip your throat out.

But the blow never comes.

Instead, the wolf turns away from you and leaps back out the broken door that it came in from. You just stand there, trembling violently and hugging yourself. Everyone in the room is now dead. You're not in danger anymore, so that part is good, but what the hell?

It takes several minutes before you're able to coax yourself to move again. You step outside of the room, and that's when you find Avery lying in a pool of blood. The wolf got her too, apparently. You clasp a hand over your mouth, staring down at your dead friend, who did nothing more than get you a waitressing job to help you out of a jam.

But you can't stand here mourning her. You have a

feeling that if you do, you'll end up just as dead as Avery.

Turn to Chapter 54 (page 130)

54

Are you the only one left alive?

Before you can check for other survivors of the wolf's rampage, you hear footsteps coming from down the hallway. A second later, you see the silhouette of a man, and when he gets closer, you realize that it is Carson, the butler. He's limping, his hair is mussed, the white bowtie has unraveled, and when you see the streaks of blood on his white shirt, you are sure the wolf got him too.

"Carson," you gasp. "Are you badly hurt?"

"I... I'm okay," he manages.

You look him up and down to figure out where he's bleeding from, but you don't see any wounds. He must have come across one of the victims and gotten their blood on him, possibly trying to revive them. Well, he was sure right about you being in danger.

"Are you okay, Sloan?" he asks you.

You nod mutely.

"Everyone else in the house is dead," he says,

answering your only question. "I hid in a closet until the wolf was gone."

"It's gone?"

"Yes," he confirms. "It... it took off into the night. I'm not sure where it went, but I don't think we're in any danger anymore."

You nod again, your legs wobbling beneath you.

Carson notices that you are on the brink of collapse. He puts an arm around your shoulders and leads you into another of the many rooms, where he sits you down on a plush leather sofa. You hug your body, rocking back and forth. You're shaking badly, and you're not sure if you'll ever be able to stop. You thought for sure that the wolf was going to kill you.

"What now?" you finally ask.

"I think," he says quietly, "that we should get the hell out of here."

"What about the police?"

He shakes his head firmly. "Sloan, I don't have to tell you that some bad shit was going on in the house. The police will show up eventually, but I think it's better for both of us if we don't get involved."

"So you're saying we should just leave this house with a bunch of dead bodies left behind?"

"That's *exactly* what I'm saying."

You study Carson's face. It's hard not to trust somebody so incredibly handsome. Also, he is much more familiar with the occupants of this house than you are— it probably wasn't even his first dinner party. He knows what he's talking about.

Then again, there are people *dead* in this house. You

have to do something about it. You can't just leave them behind! Can you?

To call the police, turn to Chapter 55 (page 133)

To leave without calling the police, turn to Chapter 56 (page 137)

55

You have to call the police. Even though you haven't been 100% law abiding in your life (to say the least), there's no way you can leave a house full of dead people without contacting the proper authorities.

"This is a mistake," Carson warns you.

"You might be correct," you admit, "but it's the right thing to do."

He lets out a long sigh. God, he is sexy when he's exasperated—but given what you went through, it seems likely that hooking up is off the table tonight. "There's a phone in the sitting room. I'll take you there."

Carson leads you to another room, which you guess is the sitting room. It contains a mahogany desk with a cordless phone resting on it. While you pick up the receiver and type in the three digits, Carson wanders out of the room. For whatever reason, he does not want to be present for this call. You wonder if he has some legal problems himself and would prefer to avoid the police.

"911, what's your emergency?"

You hesitate. Even though you've had time to think about what you're going to say, now that you're faced with the operator, your mouth goes dry. "Um, I have an emergency."

"Yes...?"

"I was at a dinner party and this... well, a wolf came in and ate everyone."

There's a long silence on the other end of the line. "Is this a joke?"

"No," you say quickly. "It's not a joke. It was... well, the wolf didn't actually *eat* everyone. He just mauled most of them. But either way, everyone is dead."

Another long silence. Geez, is it really so hard to believe that a wolf came in and ate like a dozen people?

The operator finally connects you to the police, and you have to repeat the entire story, meeting equal amounts of disbelief. But you eventually convince them it's not an elaborate prank, and they say they're sending over a car right away.

After you hang up, the house seems so silent. Too silent. You peek your head outside the sitting room door, and find the hallway to be empty. "Carson?"

No answer.

You step outside, scanning left and right. But there's no sign of Carson anywhere.

"Carson?" you call out again.

There's only silence. Could he have left? He did say it was a mistake to call the police. It seems that he does not want to be present when they arrive.

You return to the sitting room to wait. About half an

hour later, you hear the doorbell ring. When you answer the door, there are two officers standing in front of you. You let them in.

"Thank God you're here!" you say. "As I said on the phone, I was working as a waitress at this dinner party, and then this wolf got loose and ended up killing everyone."

The two officers exchange looks. "Would you please show us the bodies?"

You lead them inside. As they follow you, you get a bad feeling that Carson might have been right. Maybe calling the police *was* a mistake. But this is the choice you made, and it's too late to choose otherwise.

You bring the officers to the room where all the carnage took place. Both of them let out audible gasps when they see all the dead bodies. It is only after several seconds have passed that one of them recovers enough to speak to you.

"Sloan Morrison," he says. "You are under arrest for murder."

What?

How could they possibly think that you're the one who killed all these people? You don't even have fangs or claws! But now they're snapping handcuffs on your wrists and leading you out of the house to their police car. As they load you into the police car, you hear several more sets of sirens in the distance.

Mr. Wentworth, unsurprisingly, had a lot of powerful friends who want to see someone pay for his murder. The trial is short and frustrating, and at the end of it, you are sentenced to 16 life terms in prison.

On the plus side, at least you don't have to worry about the rent ever again.

THE END

Want to try for a different ending? Turn back to Chapter 1 (page 1)!

56

CARSON SEEMS TO KNOW WHAT HE'S TALKING ABOUT. If he says you shouldn't call the police, you're going to trust him on that.

"So what should we do now?" you ask.

"There's no electronic record of you ever being here," he says. "They made sure of that, so it wouldn't get tracked back to them when you disappeared. The best thing to do is to go home and pretend like none of this ever happened. Since everyone is dead, I'll be able to unlock and open the gates so we can get out."

You hold out your hands, which are still shaking terribly. "I don't think I can make the drive right now. I'll probably go careening off the edge of the mountain."

Carson looks at you thoughtfully with his gray eyes. "I can drive you home in your car. My car is a loaner from Mr. Wentworth anyway."

You promised Blair that you wouldn't let anyone else

drive her car, but you're pretty sure Carson will be a good driver. After all, he's so handsome.

You make your way to the front door. With each step, you leave behind bloody footprints. You wipe your shoes really well on the welcome mat, knowing Blair will be furious if you track blood into the car. You unlock the front door, and when you step outside, Carson hesitates.

"What's wrong?" you ask.

You follow Carson's gaze to the sky. There's a full moon out, although there's still a bit of mist keeping it from being as luminous as full moons can sometimes be.

"Pretty, isn't it?" you say.

Carson lets out a grunt. There's an expression on his face that seems almost pained. He rakes a hand through his thick white-blond hair, and for a moment, it looks like his hand is shaking as badly as yours are.

"What's wrong?" you ask him.

"Nothing," he says in a gruff voice. "Let's get to your car. *Hurry*."

He seems to be struggling to walk as the two of you make your way to Blair's Audi. When you get there, you see four deep slashes across the passenger's side door, which resemble claw marks.

"Oh man!" you moan. "Blair's going to *kill* me!"

Carson seems utterly uninterested in the claw marks on the car. He fumbles to get the driver's side door open, then collapses into the seat. Once you are both inside, he takes a few deep breaths, gripping the steering wheel.

"Okay," he says, "let's go."

"Are you sure you're okay?"

"Now I am."

You're not quite sure what that means, but you still don't think you're up for a drive, so you let him take the lead. Sure enough, after you get on the road, he seems a lot better. You sit together, listening to the sounds of the pop station on the radio while you try to figure out what the hell you're going to tell Blair about her car.

"Did you know?" you ask him. "I mean, that they were…?"

"Cannibals?" Carson finishes for you.

You try to smile, but your lips feel like rubber. "Yeah. That."

"I didn't know for sure," he says. "Not until tonight. But I did know that…"

"Know what?"

"I knew they were bad people. Really bad people."

"So if you knew that," you say, "why did you take a job as their butler?"

Carson glances at you out of the corner of his eye, as if deciding whether or not to trust you. "Something had to be done."

You don't quite know what he means by that. Was he somehow responsible for the carnage that took place this evening? In some ways, he seems just as frazzled as you are. But in other ways, he was so calm at the house and knew exactly what to do.

But he couldn't have been responsible for all that. You can't imagine Carson letting a wolf loose in the house. After all, if he had done that, the wolf could have easily killed you both, in addition to the Adventurous

Eaters Club. You're sure he wouldn't have taken that chance.

But are you actually sure? The truth is, you hardly know this man at all.

Turn to Chapter 57 (page 141)

57

YOU DON'T TALK MUCH DURING THE TWO-HOUR DRIVE back home. When Carson pulls over in front of your building, you are overcome with relief. It suddenly hits you that you escaped death tonight. If things had unfolded differently, who knows what would have happened? The night barely feels real.

"Well, here we are," Carson announces.

"Thank you for driving me," you say, "and for getting me out of there in one piece."

"Of course," he says.

You sit there together in the car for about sixty seconds, staring at each other. Despite everything, you almost wish he would kiss you. After all you've been through tonight, you have a connection to this man. Also, he's hot.

"I'll check on you tomorrow," he promises. "Make sure you're okay."

"You swear?"

"I swear."

His words give you a warm feeling in your stomach. He's going to check on you. That sounds promising. Except how will he check on you? He doesn't have your phone number. You open your mouth to offer him your digits, but before you can, he gets out of the car and races down the street, disappearing down the alley next to your building.

What a strange man. What a strange, strange, sexy man.

He left the keys in the ignition, so you pull them out to return them to Blair. You get out of the car, wincing at the damage from the claw marks. Unfortunately, you didn't get the money you needed tonight, but almost dying puts things in perspective. One way or another, you'll figure things out. There's always that website where you can learn about fans and A/C units.

You shiver in the frigid night air. The mist in the sky has cleared, and the full moon shines brightly overhead, illuminating your path to the door. You feel safe right now. You might have been in danger earlier tonight, but that danger is over.

And then, just as you are entering the building, the howl of what sounds like a wolf cuts through the air. You shiver, remembering the carnage back at the dinner party, and then slip inside, locking the door behind you. It's probably a stray dog, but better safe than sorry.

When you get upstairs, you unlock the door to your apartment, wanting only to collapse into your bed and sleep for the next twelve hours. But when you get inside, before you even turn on the lights, you suddenly sense that you're not alone.

"Hello?" you call out.

You flick on the light switch and gasp when you see the stranger standing in the middle of your living room. It takes you a moment to recognize the bushy beard and unkempt hair.

It's the hitchhiker. And his lips are pulled back into a maniacal grin.

"Hello, Sloan."

Before you can react, his hands are around your neck, squeezing. You open your mouth to scream, but no sound comes out. You're dying. He's killing you, and you have no idea why. All you know is that your story is coming to an end.

Turn to the Epilogue (page 144)

EPILOGUE
JASPER

You might know me as the hitchhiker. But hitchhiking was never my intention, only incidental.

You see, we've met before, Sloan. You don't remember me because my life was different back then. *I* was different. That was when I had Lorna at my side.

Before you killed her.

I'm sure you don't think you were responsible for Lorna's death. You probably thought you were a hero when you walked into that zoo with the master keys you stole and started freeing all the animals. *They will no longer be your prisoners!* was what you shouted with your fist in the air.

You argued in court that you didn't free any animals that were likely to harm people. You left the cages of the lions, tigers, and bears well secured. What's the harm in letting out a few zebras or an emu?

Tell that to my wife.

But no, you can't.

Because she was trampled to death. By a giraffe.

You are responsible for Lorna's demise. And the giraffe, of course, although I have already eliminated her. If not for your careless actions, my wife would still be here right now instead of a box of ashes. It is a travesty of justice that you are walking free while she is gone, and I intend to correct that error.

You thought you were making choices to outsmart me. You avoided me for a little while. But eventually, I caught up to you.

And now I will finish you.

After you are dead, I will take out the bag containing the deadly nightshade berries that I have been carrying around. I will swallow them, lie down beside Lorna's ashes, and then I will join her on the other side.

I'll see you soon, my love.

THE END

Want to try for a different ending? Turn back to Chapter 1 (page 1)!

58

_____

It would be very stupid to confront a group of people who were about to eat you. God knows what they're capable of. Better to just keep moving until you're safely out of the house.

You follow Avery down the hallway, finally reaching the foyer. From here, the front door is just a stone's throw away. You start towards it, but Avery gestures wildly to you.

"Don't go out that way!" she warns you. "That's what they'll be *expecting*. Let's go out through the back, like I said."

Avery is one of your closest friends, but you're not sure if you should follow her. The front door is *right there*, and your car isn't too far away. If you go out through the back, you're going to be in the middle of nowhere. It seems risky.

"Trust me," Avery says, "Mr. Wentworth is extremely smart. He's probably already got someone waiting for you outside the front door. If you try to get out that way, they'll knock you out and bring you right back into the house."

Avery has worked here before and seems to know both this house and your employer better than you do. If she says going out through the back is safer, maybe you should just follow her.

To go out through the front, turn to Chapter 60 (page 151)

To follow Avery to the back, turn to Chapter 59 (page 148)

59

AVERY IS ONE OF YOUR CLOSEST FRIENDS, AND SHE wouldn't steer you wrong. If she says going through the back is the safest way to get out, you're better off following her.

You keep close to Avery as you hurry through the first floor of the house. It looked cavernously large from the outside, but now that you're inside, it feels endless. There are a million hallways and twists and turns. If you didn't have Avery, you'd be completely lost. Thank God she's here to guide you.

It feels like you've been walking for miles. You stop for a moment to catch your breath. "Is it much farther?"

She hesitates only a moment. "Not much," she assures you.

She takes you down another hallway, and now you're getting concerned, because you definitely recognize that portrait of Mr. Wentworth. You've been here before—you know it. But how is that possible? Are you going around in circles?

You hope Avery knows what she's doing. Maybe you would have been better off just going out the front door, but it's far too late for that. You'd never find your way back there.

Finally, you reach a white door with an ornate bronze doorknob. Avery reaches over to turn the knob and then pushes the door open. And….

Wait. This is *the dining room*.

Mr. Wentworth is sitting at one of the place settings, his hands folded in front of him. His gray hair had become slightly disheveled when he was first coming after you, but now it's been smoothed back into place. When he sees you, he gets to his feet.

He's holding a knife in his right hand.

You look from Mr. Wentworth to Avery, your head spinning. What's going on here? Avery lowers her eyes, unable to look at you. "I'm so sorry, Sloan."

"What?" you croak.

"They offered me *so* much money," she says, almost frantically. "Enough to get me out of debt, with enough left over for me to buy a loft. You *know* I've always wanted a loft, Sloan."

It hits you like a ton of bricks. Avery *knew* these people were cannibals the whole time. She knew they were going to eat you, and she was fine with it! She sold you out! You turn around, ready to bolt, but the door to the dining room is now closed. You reach for the knob and discover it doesn't turn.

"Don't be upset, Sloan," Mr. Wentworth says to you as he comes around the dining table. "It's a great honor to be served by the Adventurous Eaters Club. As you can see, we only choose the *creme de la creme* of animals. And now you're going to join them on our wall for all eternity."

He looks at you like he expects you to thank him. Instead, you spit in his face. Unperturbed, he wipes away the glob of saliva.

"It's best to just let this happen," he says. "All of the animals we've dined on have put up some amount of fight, but it's always easiest on them if they don't."

Fight—yes, that's what you should do. You've got to fight. Except… how? You don't have a weapon. The place settings only have butter knives, which really shouldn't even be called knives at all. And it's now two against one.

Before you can even weigh your options, Mr. Wentworth lunges at you. He draws the blade across your neck, and if you ever did have a chance at escape, it is now gone. You fall to your knees, choking on whatever words you were going to say.

If only you had gone out the front door. Everything would have been different.

THE END

Want to try for a different ending? Turn back to Chapter 1 (page 1)!

OR to come back as a ghost, turn to Chapter 66 (page 169)

60

THE FRONT DOOR IS RIGHT THERE. YOU'D BE STUPID *NOT* to go out that way. Even if somebody is waiting for you, all you have to do is get to your car, which you parked right next to the house.

"Listen," you say to Avery, "I'm going out the front. It will be fine."

"But Sloan—"

You're not listening, though. Given that there are cannibals on your tail, the last thing you want is to stand around debating how to get out of this house. You're going out the front door, and that's all there is to it.

You hurry toward the door, Avery following close behind, still protesting. You pull the door open, you step outside, and...

Nothing.

Nobody is lying in wait with a knife or gun. Nobody is ready to pounce. It doesn't look like there's anyone here at all. The night is completely quiet.

"See?" you say triumphantly to Avery. "There's nobody here."

She opens her mouth as if to object, but before she can, a figure emerges from the shadows. You watch in horror as the intruder slams a rock down against Avery's skull. Her legs give out, and she falls to the ground, unconscious, a drop of blood trickling down her temple.

You raise your eyes to confront Avery's assailant, and you nearly choke when you see who is standing before you. It's Carson, the butler.

Oh God, Avery was right. Mr. Wentworth did send a henchman out here to wait for you. Now Avery is unconscious, and Carson is going to kill you and bring you back for dinner. If only you had made a different choice.

You turn around, ready to flee, but before you can, Carson reaches out and wraps his fingers around your arm. His grip is like a vise.

"Sloan!" he says. "Wait!"

"Let me go!" you shout, trying desperately to shake him off.

"I'm not going to hurt you. I swear."

Is he serious? He just knocked your friend unconscious with a rock, and now he's telling you he's not going to hurt you? He must think you are the dumbest person on the planet.

"Listen to me," he pleads. "I only knocked Avery out because she was leading you to Mr. Wentworth. I was trying to warn you about her—about all of them."

Something in his voice makes you stop struggling. Is there any chance he could be telling the truth? Avery is a good friend, but everything that has happened here tonight has been really sketchy, especially when she didn't want you to go out the front door. It doesn't seem completely out of the question that she was in on it the whole time.

After all, she knew how desperate you were for money. She also knows that you don't have many friends or family and would be unlikely to be missed. If she were trying to think of the perfect person to offer up to a bunch of cannibals, it's hard to imagine your name wouldn't have topped the list.

"Wentworth paid her to get you to come here," he says, confirming your fears. "I'm sure he offered her a bundle."

Avery's body is lying crumpled on the ground. You're still not sure if you believe him.

"Did *you* know what was going on?" you ask Carson.

He rubs his jaw. He looks so handsome in the moon-light. Nobody that good-looking could be evil. Could they?

"I had my suspicions," he admits. "But I didn't know for sure. Not until tonight."

"I see…"

"We've got to get out of here." His gaze darts over to your car, which is less than fifty feet away. You're sure you could span the distance in a few seconds. "But not in your car."

"Why not?"

"You need to get through the gates," he explains. "But they're not going to just open them and let you leave."

153

He makes a good point. You'll never be able to drive out of here if nobody opens the gate for you. "So how do we get out of here?"

"I've been checking the perimeter. Looking for imperfections. I found a place where one of the bars was loose, and I managed to work it free. We can sneak out through there."

"Where?"

He points to an area on the estate that is almost consumed by branches and shrubbery. It looks like exactly the kind of place that would be perfect to murder somebody.

"Um," you say, "I don't know…"

"Sloan." His eyes are big and serious. You can't help but think he has unfairly long eyelashes for a man. "Mr. Wentworth is likely guarding the controls for the gate, so unless he's dead, this is the *only* way out of the estate right now. If you don't come with me, you won't leave here alive. You have to trust me."

Except… can you trust him? You only met this man tonight, and he's already knocked your friend unconscious. That does not bode well for what will happen if you follow him into the woods.

Then again, if he wanted to attack you, he had his chance. And he's the only person in the house who warned you about the danger you were facing.

To follow Carson, turn to Chapter 64 (page 163)

To go to your car, turn to Chapter 61 (page 155)

61

YOU'RE NOT ABOUT TO TRUST A MAN WHO JUST knocked your friend unconscious with a rock, no matter how hot he is. You're certainly not going to follow him into the wilderness when your car is literally *right there*. Besides, whatever the people in this house will do to you pales in comparison to what Blair will do if you come back without her car.

"Sorry," you say to Carson, "but I'm going to find a way out of here in my car."

His face creases in concern. "Please reconsider. You'll never get out of here in thàt car."

"I'll be fine," you assure him.

He doesn't make a move to stop you as you walk over to the Audi. You hit the button on the fob to unlock the door, and then slide into the driver's seat. After you close and lock the door, you already feel safer. You definitely made the right decision.

You make your way down the driveway, the reverse

of what you did when you came here earlier. If only you had turned around when you came to the gate, but it's too late to think about that. The important thing is that you're going to get out of here in one piece.

Or at least, that's what you think until you get to the gate.

You were hoping that, despite what Carson said, there would be some sort of automatic device that would sense your car and open the gate, but that clearly isn't going to happen. These gates are not going to open without help.

Crap.

While you're weighing your options, a movement in one of the bushes catches your eye. Immediately, your heart speeds up. What was that? Is somebody following you? Is that Carson? Or is it just your imagination?

Either way, you've got to get out of here—*now*.

You've got two choices. You could get out of the car and attempt to open the gates manually. Alternatively, you could ram the gate with your car and hope that it's enough to bust them open.

You're not too jazzed about getting out of the car, but ramming the gate is going to cause significant damage to the fender, and Blair will not be cool about that, especially since you're not returning home with rent money. But what else can you do? Now that Carson is gone, there's no other way out of here.

To ram the gate with your car, turn to Chapter 62 (page 158)

To get out of the car and try to open the gate manually, turn to Chapter 63 (page 160)

62

There's no way in hell you're getting out of this car with cannibals lurking on the premises. The Audi is really well made. You bet you can bust through whatever lock is on the gate if you go at it fast enough, and the car will probably be fine. You bet it won't even get scratched, and even if it does... well, Blair will have to deal with it.

You back up, hoping to build up some momentum. When you get a decent distance from the gate, you say a quiet prayer, drop your foot onto the gas pedal, and push it all the way down.

The car jerks forward. You've never put the pedal to the metal before, and it feels *good*. You grip the steering wheel with both hands, your eyes pinned on the gate ahead of you. The bars are iron and appear sturdy, but the lock won't stand up to a car going this fast. No way.

You hold your breath as the fender makes contact with the iron gate.

It takes you a split second to realize how wrong you

were. The Audi is no match for whatever lock was holding the gate together. Worse, you realize you forgot to put on your seatbelt, so when the car stops short, your body goes flying through the windshield, landing unceremoniously on the hood. Your last thought before your skull breaks the glass is that Blair is going to *kill* you when she sees what you did to her car.

The first piece of good news is that you are alive but completely unconscious when the cannibals descend on you. The second piece of good news is that it will be far too late for Blair to kill you when she sees what you did to her car.

THE END

Want to try for a different ending? Turn back to
Chapter 1 (page 1)!

63

THERE'S NO WAY YOU'RE RAMMING BLAIR'S CAR INTO that gate. Those cannibals might be trying to kill you, but so will Blair if you return the Audi with the fender smashed in.

Your only chance of getting out of here alive is if you get out of the car and open the gate manually. You don't see any sort of lock, so maybe all you need to do is give the gate a good shove, and it will open up. That's what you hope, anyway.

You say a silent prayer, then you climb out of the car. When you first got outside, the sky had been hazy, but the haze has cleared momentarily, and the full moon peeks out again. That will make it easier to see what you're doing, at least.

As you walk over to the gate, you hear rustling coming from the bushes again. Your stomach churns slightly, but you try not to think about it. You're going to be out of here in a few minutes anyway. You just need to figure out how to get this gate open.

When you get close to the opening between the two sides of the gate, you don't see any sort of lock. You grab one of the bars with your hand and give it a firm shake—it doesn't budge.

This is not good.

You grasp another bar with your other hand, and this time you push against both bars with the entire weight of your body, grunting with the effort. After a minute of this, you realize it's hopeless. There hasn't been even a millimeter of give.

That's when the rustling sound gets louder.

You turn around, alarmed. Your heart leaps at the sight of Mr. Davenport Wentworth standing by your car. He is smiling patiently at you, his arms folded across his chest.

"Sloan, Sloan, Sloan," he says. "Where do you think you're going?"

"I…" Your throat feels so dry, it's hard to even get any words out. "I'd like to go home, that's all. Please."

"But Sloan." He cocks his head to the side. "We have your services reserved for the entire night. You can't leave *early*."

The rustling coming from the bushes is now disturbingly loud. You watch in horror as four of the other dinner guests emerge from the shrubbery. One of them is that man with the European accent, who is holding a spear in his right hand and licks his lips when he sees you.

You never should've gotten out of your car. If only you had rammed the gate like you were considering.

The man with the spear hurls it at you. It misses—

barely—and wedges itself in the hood of the car. You let out a scream—Blair is going to *kill* you if you come home with a spear stuck in the car.

Panicked that the car might sustain more damage, you try to get back to the driver's side door. But you should have worried less about the car and more about yourself. Those old people are surprisingly light on their feet, and before you can reach the handle of the door, they pounce. You had thought your life couldn't get any worse, but you had no idea that tonight you were going to be cooked and eaten by the Adventurous Eaters Club.

But on the plus side, you turn out to be delicious.

THE END

Want to try for a different ending? Turn back to Chapter 1 (page 1)!

64

You're not sure why, but you trust Carson. There's something earnest about him that makes you think he truly cares about you and wants to save you.

"All right," you say. "Let's go."

The two of you dash in the direction of the wooded part of the estate. Carson would probably move faster without you, but he's deliberately matching his pace to yours. Whenever you start to fall behind, he slows down to let you catch up. At one point, you stumble, and he grabs your arm to steady you.

Just as you're getting closer to the wooded area, you see a flash of movement near one of the trees you're approaching. Carson swivels his gaze to the side as he slows to a halt, ten feet shy of the tree. He puts a protective hand on your shoulder.

"Who's there?" he calls out.

For a moment, there's only silence. But then a familiar man emerges from behind the tree. You recognize his bushy, graying beard immediately.

It's the hitchhiker.

"I'm sorry to scare you." His hands are raised in the air in a gesture of surrender. "But I don't mean you any harm."

Carson's eyes narrow. "What are you doing then?"

"I came to *warn* you." The hitchhiker glances to the side nervously. "The people in the house… They know your plan. They know how you're trying to escape, and they're waiting for you."

Carson sucks in a breath. "No. That's impossible."

"I overheard them talking," the hitchhiker insists. "I swear, they're going to kill you. Both of you."

Carson stares at him, shaking his head. He appears to debate the situation, but then he comes to a conclusion: "You're lying."

"Lying?" the hitchhiker repeats. "Why would I lie? What would I have to gain?"

"I genuinely don't know." Carson nods his head in the direction of the gate. "But I don't believe anyone is waiting for us."

For a moment, a slice of light passes over the hitch-hiker's face as the mist around the moon clears for a second then returns.

"Listen to me." The hitchhiker turns to you, apparently realizing Carson is a lost cause. "If you follow him, they're going to kill you. I *promise*. I found another way out, and that's the only way you're getting out of here."

"Don't listen to him, Sloan," Carson growls. "I don't know what his game is, but he's misleading you. Come with me, and we'll get out of here together. I'll make sure you're safe."

You look between the two men, unsure what to do. They are both strangers. Who are you supposed to believe?

To follow the hitchhiker, turn to Chapter 65 (page 166)

To follow Carson, turn to Chapter 67 (page 172)

65

THE HITCHHIKER SEEMS SO CERTAIN ABOUT THE cannibals lying in wait. Carson might not believe him, but you do. After all, why would he lie?

"You know another way out?" you ask the hitchhiker.

"Yes," he says without hesitation. "It's not far from here."

You turn back to Carson, who is frowning down at you. "I'm sorry," you say to him. "But I think he might be right. I think they're waiting for us."

"I really wish you'd reconsider, Sloan," he says softly. "I'm your only chance to get out of here in one piece. I mean that."

For a moment, you almost consider changing your mind. But no, it's too late. This is the path you have chosen.

"Come on, Sloan." The hitchhiker gestures for you to follow him. "I'll show you the way."

You follow the hitchhiker along the side of the mansion. As you walk beside him, you cast a look over your shoulder and find that Carson is staring after you. But after a few minutes, he disappears from view.

"Your friend seemed worried about you," the hitchhiker remarks. "Do you think he'll follow us?"

"He's not my friend," you correct him. "I only met him tonight. We're basically strangers."

"Is that so?" the hitchhiker asks. "Interesting. So I guess that means he isn't *that* concerned about you."

The moon disappears behind some clouds again, and the ground darkens. You suck in a breath. "Are we almost there?"

"Almost."

The hitchhiker continues to lead you around the mansion, and then through a patch of trees and bushes. Finally, you come to a stop near the gate. Unfortunately, you don't see any defects in the gate that you can climb through.

"I don't understand," you say. "How are we supposed to get out of here?"

"Actually…" A smile spreads across the hitchhiker's lips. "You're not."

Before you can absorb his words, he reaches out and wraps his fingers around your throat. You try to scream, hoping Carson might hear and rush to your rescue, but the hitchhiker's fingers have blocked your windpipe. All you can do is let out a strangled croak, one last syllable before your life comes to a close:

"*Why?*"

THE END

Want to try for a different ending? Turn back to
Chapter 1 (page 1)!

66

After being murdered in this house, your soul is far too restless to go to any sort of afterlife. After a brief negotiation at the Pearly Gates, you find yourself back in the exact spot where you were killed. Except now you are a ghost.

Interestingly, it turns out you're not the only one haunting this house. Many other animals are walking around the hallways, some far more exotic than the ones whose photos were on the wall in the dining room. There is one creature that seems to be a cross between a rooster, a cat, and maybe a dragon.

While you are getting your bearings, another creature comes bounding toward you. This one looks almost like an ape, except covered in white fur. It has huge white fangs that look like they could rip your throat out. Actually, that probably can't happen now that you're a ghost, but who really knows? You can't be killed but maybe you can be *double-killed*. Either way, it makes you nervous that this monster is rushing toward you, and you instinctively take a step back.

But then it stops short, just before double-killing you.

"Hello," the creature says. "My name is Nicole."

"Uh, hi," you say. "I'm Sloan."

You now recognize the creature as the abominable snowman (snowwoman?) pictured in the dining room. She looked quite formidable in her photo, but right now, she seems very down-to-earth and lovely.

"How long have you been here?" you ask her.

"Years," Nicole says sadly. "I used to live with my husband out on the mountain, but then I was captured and killed. I've been haunting this house ever since."

"Haunting the house?" That idea appeals to you. "What does that involve?"

"Mostly little things," she says. "You can knock paintings off the walls or make scary noises. Sometimes, if you get really excited, you can slime things. If you do too much, though, they call these four guys with power packs to come over and get rid of you. They put you in this containment unit, and you have to wait for the EPA to let you out. It's kind of a pain."

"That sucks," you comment. "So basically, you just hang around, moving paintings?"

"Pretty much."

Nicole is right. There isn't much to do in this house. You explore the place a bit and discover Mr. Wentworth sitting in his study, using his computer. He looks very absorbed in whatever he is doing.

You walk around the side of his desk to look at his computer screen. As it turns out, he is on that OnlyFans site that you had been looking into to earn extra money, and…

Oh God, that site does not have *anything* to do with home cooling units! Wow. You're lucky you didn't have to resort to *that*.

Actually, being a ghost isn't so bad. You've got this big house to rattle around in, and you don't even have to pay rent.

THE END

Want to try for a different ending? Turn back to
Chapter 1 (page 1)!

67

THERE'S SOMETHING ABOUT THAT HITCHHIKER THAT YOU just don't trust, so you decide to follow Carson instead.

"Sorry," you tell the hitchhiker. "I'm going with Carson."

"Are you sure?" he presses you. "I'm telling you, this is going to be a mistake."

"It won't be a mistake," Carson says firmly. "I'll keep you safe, Sloan."

That's good enough for you.

You leave the hitchhiker behind, walking beside Carson through the wooded area. He seems so confident about where he's going, like he has planned this out very carefully. There's clearly something about him that he's not telling you, but this is not the time for questions. You've got to get out of here before it's too late.

After walking for a few minutes, you arrive at the gate. Sure enough, there is a missing bar and a space just wide enough for you to fit through. He was telling the truth. Even more promising, it doesn't seem like anyone from the mansion is lying in wait.

"Ladies first," he says.

You squeeze through the hole, and he follows right after. As you continue walking, you start to worry about what is going to happen next. You've escaped the estate, but you're still stuck on Peyton's Peak, in the middle of nowhere.

"How will I get home?" you ask.

"I've got a car parked about a mile from here."

He has a car already waiting outside the estate? That means he really was planning for all this. A million questions are running through your head, and you can't wait another minute to get answers. When you reach a clearing in the woods, you grab Carson's arm, stopping him in his tracks.

"Wait," you say. "You told me you didn't know what they were doing, but then how come you have a car waiting?"

Carson grits his teeth and looks up at the sky, then back at my face. "Can we discuss this later, please?"

"You've got to tell me *something*," you insist. "I have blindly followed you this far, but it's not fair that I have no idea what's going on."

The shadows on Carson's face disappear as the mist in the sky shifts, revealing the full moon in all its glory. His shoulders rise and fall, and for a moment, he looks almost as if he is in physical pain.

"Sloan," he says urgently. "We can't talk about this right now, okay?"

"But—"

Your protests are cut off by the loud groan emitted from Carson's lips. He doubles over as if he has food poisoning, and then he lets out a noise that's something between a moan and a growl. What is going on here?

You take a few steps back as Carson falls to his knees. And then onto all fours. He lets out another guttural sound, and then he claws at his shirt, finally ripping it open. You expected a gleaming six-pack of abs under that shirt, but instead, his abdomen is covered with a thick layer of brown and white fur.

And then, all of a sudden, the fur is everywhere. It's covering his entire body, and his hands have morphed into claws. His perfect nose and chin have turned into a snout. Then he raises his head and lets out a howl that echoes into the night.

Carson is a werewolf.

Turn to Chapter 68 (page 175)

68

"OH MY GOD!" YOU CRY. "YOU'RE A... A *WEREWOLF*?"

You didn't even know werewolves were real except in all those romance books. And you never quite understood why women were so attracted to werewolves. Although actually, right now, you do sort of get it.

Carson the werewolf stands there, breathing hard. Clearly, turning into a wolf took a lot out of him, which, you guess, makes sense. This hasn't really answered any of your questions, though. It has, in fact, only created many new and more confusing questions.

"I'm sorry I didn't tell you," he says in his gruff werewolf voice. "Most humans don't understand."

"I understand." Well, sort of. Actually, not at all.

He seems able to walk on his two hind feet. He approaches you with a tender expression on his face. "I could tell from the moment I met you that you were a lover of animals. I thought if there was anyone who could understand, it would be you."

He's right. You *do* love animals. "What were you doing working as a butler, though?"

"I only got the job last week," he explains. "My little sister vanished, and I tracked her by scent to this estate. I came here to find and rescue her. Except when I found out what they were doing here, I decided to wait for a meeting of the Adventurous Eaters Club to take all those bastards down in one fell swoop."

"Sorry if I got in the way of your plans," you say.

"I'm just glad I was there to save you," he says soberly. "I'll go back later and take care of the rest of them."

"Well..." You raise your eyes to meet his. Even though now he's a wolf, he still has sexy gray eyes with long, sooty eyelashes. "I appreciate what you did for me. I *really* appreciate it."

It's true. Carson saved your life tonight, even though he could just as easily have taken his sister-wolf and left. He looked out for you. He's a good man. Well, man-wolf.

Carson reaches for your hand. At his touch, a tingle goes through you that you haven't experienced in a long time. And you can see in his eyes that he is thinking the same thing you are.

To mate with the werewolf, turn to Chapter 71 (page 182)

To tell him you just want to be friends, turn to Chapter 69 (page 177)

69

"Listen," you say, "I think you're incredibly attractive, but this has all been a lot to absorb tonight."

"I'm sure it is," Carson agrees. "And if you don't feel like going home tonight, you're welcome to stay at my place."

"Your place?" you ask dubiously. "Where is that?"

You're not excited to stay at a werewolf's den. You assume it's some sort of weird cave.

"I have a mansion," Carson says.

"A… a mansion?"

"Yes," he confirms. "I invested in Bitcoin, and now I'm a billionaire."

The werewolf is also a *billionaire*? Wow, that might change things.

To change your mind and mate with the werewolf, turn to Chapter 71 (page 182)

To insist again that you just want to be friends, turn to Chapter 70 (page 179)

70

"ACTUALLY," YOU SAY, "I'D RATHER JUST GO HOME. IF it's all okay with you."

Carson nods. "I completely understand. I would have loved to show you my mansion, but I understand that sometimes it's just not meant to be."

You wonder if you're making a mistake, but no. As much as you like Carson, it feels like there will be some major downsides to dating a werewolf that you're not thinking of right now. It's better to remain friends.

Eventually, you reach Carson's car, which turns out to be a really cool red Jaguar. Man, you could have dated a guy with a Jaguar! Again, you wonder if you're making a mistake, but it's too late now. You've already made the decision.

Carson drives you back to your apartment building. By the time you get there, he has morphed back into his human form. He smiles at you as you sit in the car by the entrance to your building.

"I'd like to pay you what Avery promised for the

evening," he says, pulling his wallet out of his back pocket. You're not sure how his pants stayed intact during the transition from human to wolf and then back to human, but there might be some things you're not meant to understand.

"You don't have to give me any money," you protest.

"I want to," he insists. "Besides, I'm a billionaire, remember?"

Ugh, way to rub it in.

He gives you even more than what Mr. Wentworth owed you—enough to pay Blair this month's rent and next and then some. That will tide you over for a little while and give you some breathing room. "What about my car?"

"I'm going to go back and take care of the rest of the Adventurous Eaters Club," he says. "When I'm done with them and have freed my sister, I'll be able to open the gates and drive your car back here."

"Thank you, Carson."

He reaches for your hand and kisses the back of it. What a sweet guy. And you're definitely going to keep up with this friendship. After all, it seems like it might come in handy to know a billionaire werewolf.

When you get upstairs to your apartment, your head is still swimming from the events of the evening. What a narrow escape. If anything had gone differently, you could be dead right now.

"Hello, Sloan."

The disembodied voice coming from the living room startles you. You flick on the light and find Blair waiting for you in the corner of the room, fury in her eyes.

"Where's my car, Sloan?"

"Oh," you say. "Well, there was an… issue with it. But I'll have it back to you later. Later today. I promise."

She takes a step towards you, her hands balled into tight fists. "Didn't I tell you that there would be trouble if anything happened to my car? Isn't that what I said?"

"Your car is fine, Blair."

"*Then where is it?*"

"I promise, it's—"

Before you can explain, Blair picks up her selfie stick from the coffee table and comes running at you. You aren't really worried because it's just a selfie stick, but then you realize she's been planning this. She's attached some sort of razor-sharp point to the end of the stick, which impales your chest. You collapse to the floor, blood pouring from your wound, draining the life out of you.

On the plus side, you get an excellent selfie of yourself while you're dying.

THE END

Want to try for a different ending? Turn back to Chapter 1 (page 1)!

71

THE WAY CARSON IS LOOKING AT YOU, YOU JUST KNOW what he is thinking. He wants you. And you want him just as badly.

You're going to go for it.

You leap into his arms, pressing your lips against his snout. It is the best kiss you have ever had. You make out for another minute, and then you start pulling off your blouse. You expect him to rip it open the way he did with his own shirt, but instead, he backs away.

"Whoa!" he says. "What are you doing?"

Oh God, how embarrassing. You totally got your signals crossed. "I… I'm sorry. I thought you wanted to…"

"I like you, Sloan," he says seriously. "But I don't do *that*."

"You don't?"

"No." He frowns. "I plan to wait for marriage. Of course."

What? This super handsome werewolf guy is waiting for *marriage*? How is that possible?

"Oh," you say.

"I know it's a little unconventional." He shifts, a bit uncomfortable. "But I feel like with the right woman, she'll understand and want to wait like I do." He gazes at you in the moonlight. "Are you that woman, Sloan?"

"Um, sure," you say. "I can wait."

Maybe he'll change his mind.

It turns out Carson drives a pretty cool red Jaguar. He takes you back to his sprawling mansion, and when you get there, you do not make love even a little bit. You sleep in separate bedrooms until your spectacular destination wedding in the Balkans, where all the guests attending are wolves. It's a magical day, and you've never been so happy.

On your wedding night, you and Carson make love for the very first time in a castle you've reserved on a hilltop. It's every bit as amazing as you imagined it would be.

As you lie together in bed when it's over, Carson snuggles up against you. "Wow," he sighs. "That was incredible."

"Yeah. I almost want a cigarette."

He laughs. "I don't want a cigarette, but I'm starving —and you know how dangerous it is when werewolves get too hungry. I'm going to get something to eat in the kitchen."

"Hey," you say, "you just worked so hard. Let me get it for you."

"Are you kidding? I'm not going to let my bride fetch me food on our wedding night."

You consider arguing with him, but maybe you should just let him wait on you. It is your wedding night, after all.

To get the food yourself, turn to Chapter 72 (page 185)

To let Carson bring you food, turn to Chapter 73 (page 187)

72

CARSON IS SO SWEET TO OFFER TO GET YOU FOOD, BUT you're not going to allow him to wait on you hand and foot just because you're married.

"You just wait here," you tell him. "I'll bring you back a snack."

"Well, okay," he agrees. "If you insist."

"What would you like?"

He licks his lips. "A steak would be nice. With some gravy."

Fortunately, Carson never requires you to cook his steaks—he likes them raw. "You got it."

You slip out of bed, throw on an oversized T-shirt, then pad out to the kitchen in your bare feet. The lights are out, but there's a full moon outside, so you can see fine without them.

You pull the T-bone steak out of the fridge. You're not sure where the gravy is, but after checking a few cabinets, you locate it on the very top shelf. You stand on your tiptoes to grab the jar and…

It falls, smashing to bits on the floor. Of course it does.

Gravy is everywhere. It splashed all over your bare legs and now as you crouch down to try to clean it up, it gets all over your arms and you manage to cut your hand on a shard of glass. What a mess! Hopefully, this isn't some kind of omen for your marriage.

"Sloan? Everything all right in there?"

Carson's voice sounds close, like he came out of the bedroom to check out the source of the crash. You call back, "Just a little spill!"

"Let me help you clean it up!"

Before you can tell him you've got it under control, you lift your eyes and there he is—your husband. Except thanks to the full moon outside the window, he is now in wolf form.

Carson pants as he looks you over, from the gravy splashed all over your body to the bloody steak to the gash in your hand. He licks his lips, hesitating only a moment. And then...

He pounces.

It only takes a few minutes until you're in Carson's belly. If only you'd listened when he told you how dangerous werewolves could be when they're hungry...

THE END

Want to try for a different ending? Turn back to
Chapter 1 (page 1)!

73

CARSON OFFERED TO GET THE FOOD, SO YOU DECIDE TO let him. It is your wedding night, after all.

You stretch out deliciously on your silk sheets, waiting for your new husband to get the food. He is so great, and you can't wait to spend the rest of your life with him. You wonder what your children will be like.

You hear a growl from downstairs, which likely means he's turned into a wolf due to the full moon, but by the time he comes back, he's returned to his human form. And he's holding a bowl of ice cream.

"For you, my love," he says. "And it's a good thing you didn't get the food. The gravy was all the way on a top shelf, and I nearly dropped it trying to get it down."

"I wouldn't have dropped it," you insist.

He kisses you on the nose. "Of course you wouldn't have. You're perfect."

He snuggles back in bed with you while you eat the ice cream, thinking about how happy you are. Ending up here with Carson on your wedding night—well, it just feels like fate. You can't wait to spend the rest of your life with him.

THE END

Want to try for a different ending? Turn back to Chapter 1 (page 1)!

ACKNOWLEDGMENTS

As this is a short work, I'll keep this short and sweet.

Thank you to everyone who read through this and gave me advice and pointed out mistakes, including my mother, Val, Dan, Emily, and the amazing staff at JRA.

But most of all, a huge thank you to my husband, who helped me storyboard the entire plot. You're right —it *was* funnier that the abominable snowman was also a hockey player.

Made in United States
North Haven, CT
15 April 2026

10052011R00108